THE CHASE

I turned around, looked at the speedometer.

We were already going sixty-five on this dinky little city street, and Annie still had the accelerator smashed all the way to the floor.

"Three hundred and twelve horses of pure turbocharged intercooled JDM power!" Annie yelled.

"What's that mean?" I said.

"It means she's out of her mind," Marco said.

The speedometer hit ninety at the next light, a hundred and five at the third. The red car was about half a block behind us now, keeping pace.

"He's got nothing," Annie said. The next light was turning red in front of us.

"Annie, Annie, Annie!" I said. I don't know if I was more terrified of Annie's driving or of whoever was in the car behind us.

Annie didn't say anything, but when we were about a hundred yards from the light, she suddenly slammed on the brakes, cut the wheel slightly. By the time we were approaching the light, the whole car was traveling sideways at about fifty miles an hour, the tires howling like a dying dog. I was pretty sure we were going to die. Annie, however, didn't look at all worried. In fact, she was grinning, her black eyes glittering in the streetlights.

. . .

OTHER BOOKS YOU MAY ENJOY

CLUB DREAD

HUNTED: BOOK TWO

CLUB DREAD

WALTER SORRELLS

SLEUTH
SPEAK

For Sarah

SPEAK
Published by the Penguin Group
Penguin Group (USA) Inc., 345 Hudson Street, New York, New York 10014, U.S.A.
Penguin Group (Canada), 90 Eglinton Avenue East, Suite 700,
Toronto, Ontario, Canada M4P 2Y3 (a division of Pearson Penguin Canada Inc.)
Penguin Books Ltd, 80 Strand, London WC2R 0RL, England
Penguin Ireland, 25 St Stephen's Green, Dublin 2, Ireland (a division of Penguin Books Ltd)
Penguin Group (Australia), 250 Camberwell Road, Camberwell, Victoria 3124, Australia
(a division of Pearson Australia Group Pty Ltd)
Penguin Books India Pvt Ltd, 11 Community Centre, Panchsheel Park, New Delhi - 110 017, India
Penguin Group (NZ), 67 Apollo Drive, Rosedale, North Shore 0745, Auckland, New Zealand
(a division of Pearson New Zealand Ltd.)
Penguin Books (South Africa) (Pty) Ltd, 24 Sturdee Avenue,
Rosebank, Johannesburg 2196, South Africa

Registered Offices: Penguin Books Ltd, 80 Strand, London WC2R 0RL, England

First published in the United States of America by Dutton Children's Books,
a division of Penguin Young Readers Group, 2006
This Sleuth edition published by Speak, an imprint of Penguin Group (USA) Inc., 2007

10 9 8 7 6 5 4 3

THE LIBRARY OF CONGRESS HAS CATALOGED THE DUTTON CHILDREN'S BOOKS EDITION AS FOLLOWS:
Sorrells, Walter.
Club Dread / Walter Sorrells.—1st ed.
p. cm.—(Hunted ; bk 2)
Summary: When sixteen-year-old Chastity witnesses the murder of a pop star, her
hopes of settling down with her mother in San Francisco seem to disappear.
ISBN 0-525-47618-0 (hardcover)
[1. Witnesses—Fiction. 2. Murder—Fiction. 3. Mothers and
daughters—Fiction. 4. Mystery and detective stories.] I. Title.
PZ7.S7216Clu 2005 [Fic]—dc22 2005012112

Speak ISBN 978-0-14-240904-6

Printed in the United States of America

Chass Farmer *and her mother have been on the run for Chass's whole life, pursued by Kyle Van Epps, the shadowy president of a sinister corporation called Apex Global Media. They carry with them a tape recording that implicates Van Epps in a murder that happened years ago. Chass wants to have a normal life. But as long as Kyle Van Epps continues to pursue them, she and her mother will remain . . .*

. . . the hunted.

ONE

I WAS TAPING a blue piece of photocopied paper to the window of this coffeehouse called Java Monkey when a guy walked up behind me. He looked over my shoulder at the poster and then read it out loud in this kind of snotty voice.

"FEMALE SINGER-SONGWRITER LOOKING FOR BAND. BASS PLAYER, DRUMMER, KEYS NEEDED. SERIOUS PRO PLAYERS ONLY. CALL CHASS AT 415-555-2783."

I glared at him.

"You're not gonna find anybody this way," he said.

"Excuse me?" I said. "Do I know you?"

"What you'll get is losers. No serious professional musician would answer an ad like this. Plus, if they did?" He looked me up and down. "Who'd want to be in a band led by some fifteen-year-old girl?"

"First," I said, "I happen to be sixteen. And second, who made you the big expert?"

He just smirked at me.

Which was when I noticed it was Josh Emmit. *The* Josh Emmit. The Josh Emmit with the show on MTV, the Josh Emmit with all the hit records, the Josh Emmit with the line of sneakers that every girl in eighth grade is wearing this year—*that* Josh Emmit. I like to think I'm not one of these dopey girls that flips out and gets all peeing in their pants and screaming when they see somebody famous. But still. I mean it *was* Josh Emmit. I just stared at him like a moron, my mouth hanging open.

Then there was this loud pop from the road, and Josh Emmit was like, "Ow! That hurt."

Then there was another pop. Really loud.

For a second I thought maybe somebody had thrown some firecrackers at him. He had this funny look on his face, like somebody had said something to him that

4

didn't make any sense. Then he grabbed his stomach and kind of hunched over against the wall, and all this blood started leaking out between his fingers.

I started screaming. "Oh my God, somebody just shot Josh Emmit! Oh my God, somebody just shot Josh Emmit!"

But there was nobody on the street to hear me. Nobody, that is, except the guy in the front seat of the big red car that was heading off down the road away from us. Josh grabbed my hand and he goes, "Hey. Hey, kid. Take this."

I looked at the thing he was handing me. It looked like a little bar of silver. It was very heavy. The number 53 was stamped into it. I turned it over; the number 100 was stamped on the other side.

"Take it and get out of here. Before they find you."

I stopped screaming long enough to say, "Before *who* finds me?"

Down the street, the red car threw on its brakes with a loud screech. The taillights went on and the car began to back up.

Little red bubbles had started coming out of Josh Emmit's mouth, and he was making this weird noise like when you suck on a milk-shake straw after the milk shake is all gone. He was trying to say something.

"What?" I said.

He pulled me toward him. "Stop. Stop . . . the hundred," he said in this bubbly, feeble voice. He waved his hand toward the road. I could see the skyline of San Francisco down the road in the direction he was pointing. The big red car was still backing toward us, getting closer and closer. I could see sunglasses reflected in the side-view mirror.

"Huh?" I said.

"Hundred. Stop. Hundred."

"A hundred what?"

"Promise me."

The car was getting closer and closer. "I would promise if I understood you, but I just—"

Josh Emmit looked over at the car, then pressed his hand against mine, folding my fingers around the silver ingot. The car was not more than thirty yards away, closing fast. "Go," he said. "Now!"

He didn't have to tell me twice. Believe me, I know all about running for your life. So that's what I did.

Okay, so I'm only sixteen years old. That doesn't mean I'm a total dumb ass. I figured if somebody had just shot Josh Emmit for whatever it was that I was carrying in my hand, this little ingot thing, then they'd probably do something even worse to me. So after about half a block, I took this thing that he'd given me and tried to chunk it into a Dumpster. I'm not like Little Miss Future Olympic Softball Champion, so this ingot thing missed, banked off the Dumpster with this huge clang, and fell behind some boxes.

I did *not* stop to pick it up and try throwing it in the Dumpster again.

I just kept running.

TWO

WHEN I GOT home, I went in my room, took out my guitar, and played until Mom came home from work. She's a waitress, working the dinner shift, so it was kind of late by the time she showed up.

She poked her head in my room and said, "How was your day, sweetie?"

And I said, "Fine."

"Did you do your homework?"

"Yeah," I lied.

She looked at me with this funny expression on her face. "Are you okay, Chass?"

"*Fine!*" I said. The word came out a little sharp. "I'm just tired is all. I think I'm going to bed."

Mom narrowed her eyes slightly. I got up before she could start doing the parental third degree, went to my bed, and lay down for a while. I couldn't sleep. Then I got back up and went into the living room, where Mom was reading a book.

Mom looked up at me, raised one eyebrow.

"Actually?" I said.

Mom waited.

"Actually, something did happen."

After I'd explained about Josh Emmit, she said, "This is not good. This is really not good."

"I didn't know what to do," I said. "I just ran. Should I have called the police?"

She looked at me for a long time, then finally, in a very quiet voice said, "No. No, honey, you did the right thing."

It's kind of a long story—why not calling the police was the right thing. What it comes down to is that Mom and I have been on the run for a long time. Mom has information about a murder committed by a very powerful man named Kyle Van Epps, and for my entire life Van Epps has been trying to catch up with us. Every now and then, he gets close to us. When that happens we have to change our names and move to a new town on about half an hour's notice. We thought we had gotten it all worked out a few months back, but then things went bad, and we had to run again.

What happened was that Van Epps had been charged with a murder in Alabama. At the time he had been shot and was in the hospital. But while he was recuperating, his minions managed to pay off some police, intimidate some witnesses, and generally make the case against him go away. At a certain point it became clear we had to grab the tape and run again—or he'd make us go away too.

"If we had any kind of a normal life," Mom said, "going to the police would be the only right thing to do. But if you go talk to them and they start running us through the computer, they'll find that we just sprang into existence about a month ago."

"I know, I know . . ."

"I realize how hard it was for you to leave Alabama, to leave Ben. I don't want to have to do that to you again."

Ben was my sort-of boyfriend in the last town where we had lived. I sat there glumly and nodded.

"Turn on the news," Mom said. "Let's see if there's anything about it."

We were about to flip on the TV when the doorbell rang. Mom's eyes darted toward the door. It was eleven o'clock at night. You didn't usually have visitors at that hour. She went over and looked out the peephole.

"Who is it?"

"Police, ma'am. I'm looking for someone named Chass."

"Slide your ID under the door, please," Mom said.

There was a pause, then a scratchy sound. A police ID appeared from under the door.

"Somebody must have seen me at the coffeehouse," I said. My heart was racing. "What are we gonna do?"

Mom took a deep breath. "We'll let him in," Mom said softly. "Just tell him what you saw. Don't give any details. Skip the part about Josh Emmit giving you whatever it was he gave you. Just say you were putting up the poster, he walked by and got shot. You were afraid and you ran."

I nodded.

"Keep it soft focus." Mom unlocked the door, looked out through the crack. "What is it?" she said through the door.

"Inspector Jerry Wise, San Francisco Police Department. Are you Chass?"

"That's my daughter's nickname. Why?"

"I need to speak to her about a homicide that occurred this afternoon."

"Come on in," Mom said.

The inspector was a chubby little guy with a red, watchful face. He wore a suit and bright red suspenders. "Chass?" he said, holding up the blue poster I'd left on the wall of the coffeehouse that afternoon.

"I should have called," I said. "I was just . . . I was just really scared."

The inspector took out a small notepad. "You were just scared. I see. Well, how about you get unscared long enough to come down to the station and talk to me."

I looked at Mom.

"What's wrong with talking here?" Mom said.

The inspector turned his sour little eyes toward Mom. "What's wrong is, I didn't ask if she wanted to talk here."

"Well, I'm asking," Mom said. "It's eleven o'clock at night. She has to go to school in the morning."

"And this seems to you like a bigger consideration than the fact that a young man was murdered this afternoon? No, I want her down at the station."

I could see Mom thinking about it. Finally I think she decided we would end up being better off not making a scene.

Twenty minutes later I was sitting in a small, dimly lit room that smelled like stale fried chicken. Mom sat next to me, and the inspector sat across the table from me.

The first thing he did was push a piece of paper across the table. "This is just a formality," he said. "You're not under arrest; we just want you fully apprised of your rights."

I looked at the form. It said, KNOW YOUR RIGHTS at the top. Underneath it said, I UNDERSTAND I HAVE THE RIGHT TO REMAIN SILENT. Next to that was a little box. All the rest of the rights that they always read people on cop shows were listed underneath.

"Please read each line and indicate you understand it by initialing each box," Inspector Wise said. "Mom, I'd like you to initial each line too, then sign on the bottom where it says, yeah, *legal guardian.*"

"Whoa, whoa, whoa," Mom said. "What is this?"

"Like I say, just a formality." Inspector Wise smiled one of those smiles where your mouth looks friendly but your eyes don't.

I looked at Mom.

"Here's the thing, Inspector," Mom said. "Before she talks to you, I want to make something clear. Chass told me what happened. This wasn't some kind of accident. This was basically an execution. Whoever killed that poor young man is not going to be interested in having live witnesses walking around this town. So I can't let her talk to you if her name is going to become a public matter, okay? I can't have her face going out on national TV. I will not have my sixteen-year-old daughter walking around with a bull's-eye on her chest. If that's the way it's going to go down, then we'll stand up and leave right this minute."

The inspector said, "If this ever goes to trial, then she might have to testify. That's out of my hands. Being she's a juvenile and whatnot, I imagine the judge would shield her identity. But that's a long way off. For the time being, anything you say, your name, your identity, whatever, that's absolutely one hundred percent confidential. Mm-kay? We all happy now?"

I looked at Mom. She nodded. But still I had this sinking feeling about the whole thing.

I picked up the form, signed it. Mom did the same.

"So." Inspector Wise sat for about thirty seconds just looking at me. Finally he spoke again. "Just to make sure we're on the same page—we had a witness saying a young woman was taping this poster on the window of a coffeehouse called Java Monkey on Warren Street when a murder occurred this afternoon. Can you tell us about that?"

"Yes."

"What's your full name?" the inspector said to me.

"Clarissa Barber."

Inspector Wise frowned. "Clarissa? Where's Chass come from? Is that your middle name?"

"I don't have a middle name. Chass is just my nickname. It's what everybody calls me."

The inspector looked puzzled, but he just wrote it all down. "Okay," he said. "Tell me what you saw today down on Warren Street."

"Not much. I was putting up a poster. This guy came up behind me and said I wasn't going to find any decent musicians using a poster like that. I felt sort of pissed because I didn't know this guy and here he is sticking his nose in my business. And then I recognized it was Josh Emmit. About that time I hear pop pop and then this car goes screeching off. Josh falls down. After a few seconds, the car stops and starts backing up. I figured maybe they'd decided to get rid of the witness or . . . well, I didn't really know. All I knew was that whoever was in that car had just shot somebody. And I might be next. So I ran."

The inspector scratched his head. "Wait. What did Josh Emmit say to you before you ran?"

I thought about it for a second. If there was actually a witness who'd seen me there, then they'd have seen him talking to me after he got shot as well as before. I didn't want to come off like a liar. "Well, he grabbed my arm and said, 'Please help me.' Then when the car started backing toward me, he goes, 'Stop. The hundred.'"

"Stop the hundred."

"Well. I don't know if he was saying, 'Stop, period. The hundred, period.' Or 'Stop the hundred, period.'"

"I don't follow you."

"Punctuation," I said. "Was it like two sentences? *Stop. The hundred.* Or one sentence? *Stop the hundred.* See?"

Inspector Wise wrote something down in his notebook. "What does that mean—stop the hundred?"

"Beats me."

"You must have talked about it before. How do you know Josh Emmit?"

"Oh, yeah," I said. "Me and Josh have been dating secretly for a year. He takes me to all the big fashion shows in Paris and Milan, and he bought me a Cadillac Escalade and all kinds of bling bling. He rented this fabulous apartment for me and Mom." I knew he had seen our crappy little apartment, so I figured he'd get the point, that I was joking. "He's been very generous. We were going to be married as soon as I turn seventeen."

The inspector took out a stick of chewing gum, popped it in his mouth, looking at me without a trace of a smile. "Was that supposed to be sarcasm, sweetie?"

"Look, I'm just some kid," I said. "I've never talked

to him, never seen him before in my life. How would he even know me?"

"He grew up in San Francisco," the inspector said. "I'm sure he knows a lot of people here."

"Well, we just moved here a couple of months ago."

"Yeah? Where from?"

"Uh . . ." I looked at Mom. "Quincy, Ohio."

"Quincy, Quincy, Quincy." He tapped on his pad with his pen. "Nah, not familiar with that."

"You haven't missed much," Mom said.

"Mom," the inspector said, "I'm talking to the young lady."

"Two things," Mom said. "First, you are not my son, so don't call me Mom. Try sticking with 'Ms. Barber.' And second, as her legal guardian, I'll pipe up whenever I please. Are you clear on that . . . Inspector?"

The inspector looked at her for a moment then turned back to me as though Mom wasn't even in the room. "Where do you go to school?" he said.

"Wallenberg."

"Raoul Wallenberg High School?"

I nodded.

"Okay, Chass, now you say there was one person in the car. What did they look like?"

"I just saw them in the side-view mirror. All I could tell about him was that they were wearing sunglasses."

"Man or woman?"

For some reason, it was my impression it was a guy. But I couldn't be sure. "I don't know. A guy maybe?"

"A guy *maybe*."

I nodded.

"White? Black? Asian?"

I shrugged. "All I saw were sunglasses."

"Blond hair? Brown hair?" The way he was saying it, it was like he couldn't believe that I wouldn't have been able to see this.

I shook my head. "I'm telling you. I didn't see anything."

"I thought you said you saw sunglasses."

I sighed loudly.

He tapped his pencil some more, finally said, "What about the car?"

"It was red and big. Maybe like a Cadillac or a Lincoln. I don't know much about cars."

He scribbled in his notebook, reading it out in a slow, loud voice as he wrote each word. "Doesn't. Know. Much. About. Cars." Then he looked up. "You make out a license plate?"

"It was like two seconds," I said defensively.

"Mm-hm." The inspector scribbled some more and then looked up at me and said, "What do you know about Club Dread? Ever hear of it?"

"Club what?" I asked.

"Okay, so let's recap. You didn't see anything or anybody. Pop, pop, there's a red car, it drives off then suddenly backs up, Josh says, 'Stop the hundred,' and you run away."

I nodded. I still hadn't told him about the ingot that Josh had handed me. I decided to do like Mom said and not tell him about it. I was feeling like maybe I'd said too much already. I felt bad about not being more honest—but the more I talked, the more likely it was I would end up as some kind of "star witness." And the more important I was as a witness, the more likely it was that my face would end up on some TV news program. At which point Mom would get all paranoid and throw us in the car and we'd have to skip town. Which I really, really didn't want to do. I was tired of running.

"Boy, Chass," the inspector said. "That's really . . . whew! . . . quite an extensive, rich, detailed story."

"What, you want me to make something up?"

"Well, I hope you haven't been doing that already," he said.

My mom chimed in, "What's that supposed to mean?"

"What that's supposed to mean is, nobody else saw this alleged red car. All they saw was your daughter."

"There was nobody else in the street!" I said. "Of *course* nobody saw them."

"You don't have to shout, hon. I'm right here." The inspector gave me his big fake smile. "Would you excuse me for a minute?"

He left the room.

"I don't like the way this is going," Mom said. "I don't like this at all. He's treating you like a suspect."

"They always do this on TV," I said. "It's probably some kind of interrogation technique." It sounded good, but I didn't believe it.

We waited for a long time. Finally Mom got up, opened the door, looked out. "Hey! Over here! My daughter's got school in the morning." Then she slammed the door. "Asshole. He was just standing over there gabbing with somebody."

A couple minutes later Inspector Wise came back in with a cup of coffee and sat down.

"So what does Club Dread mean to you?"

"Absolutely nothing, I told you," I said.

"And so what does the hundred mean to you?"

"I would say it means the thing that comes after ninety-nine and before a hundred and one."

The inspector studied my face. "I'm asking you a serious question, hon. I know you're just trying to keep things light and all, but this is a homicide investigation. Somebody died here."

"I'm being serious. I just—the hundred? I'm as mystified as you are."

"I bet you are." Inspector Wise kept looking at me like he was sure everything I had just told him was a big fat lie.

"You wait just a minute, sir—" Mom said, jabbing her finger at him.

"Hey, look, save the outrage for someone who cares," the inspector said. "And when you get done sticking your finger in my face, you can go."

Mom blinked. "All right then."

We grabbed our purses and stood up.

Just about the time Mom's hand hit the doorknob, the inspector snapped his fingers.

"Oh, yeah," he said. "I totally forgot. One last question. What was the shiny thing you threw in the Dumpster?"

Crap. My heart sank. "Huh?" I said.

"You've told me your story. Now let me tell you the story I get from one of my witnesses. This witness sees you strike up a conversation with Josh Emmit. Then they hear the same pop pop noise you told me about. Then they see you standing there with something shiny in your hand. Something about the size of gun."

"Bull," Mom said.

"Then you went running off down the street. The witness came out, watched you run, saw you throw something shiny into a Dumpster."

"Uh . . . ," I said.

"What." The inspector stared at me. "Forget the part about dumping the gun?"

"It wasn't a gun," I said.

"Oh! It wasn't a gun. Pray tell, what was it?"

"It was like . . . sort of an ingot."

"Really!" Inspector Wise was being sarcastic.

"He handed me this little silver thing. Like an ingot. It had some numbers stamped on it."

"My witness says a gun. Not an ingot. A gun."

"Then I suppose you've recovered it," I said. "I suppose you searched the Dumpster, you found a gun that has my fingerprints on it?"

Inspector Wise just sat there.

"Me and Mom are big fans of that TV show, *CSI,*" I said. "What's that test they always do, Mom?"

"GSR," Mom said. "Stands for gunshot residue. If you fired a gun, the powder leaves a residue on your hands, proves you just fired a gun. You want to give her a gunshot residue test, Inspector? Hm?"

"A GSR wouldn't do any good by now," the inspector said, smiling thinly. "You've had plenty of time to wash your hands."

"You didn't find a gun in the Dumpster, did you?" I said.

The inspector just sat there, looking at me with his sour little eyes, chewing away on his stick of gum.

"You girls have a nice night," he said finally. "But don't get comfortable, Chass. This isn't over yet."

When we got home Mom and I had a huge fight. "We have to leave right now," Mom said. "He's going to start poking around. And when he does, he's going to find out that our identities are bogus."

"I don't want to leave," I said.

"What do you mean?" Mom said. "When it's time to leave, it's time to leave."

I shook my head. "I've been running all my life. Every time somebody looks at you funny, we grab our bags, we hop in the car, and we shove off. I'm sick of it!"

"I don't make the rules," Mom said. "This is just how it is. This is how we stay alive."

"I didn't *do* anything," I said. "He can't say I did anything, because I didn't. Whoever that guy in the car was, they'll find him and they'll put him away, and that will be that."

"Did you listen to a word he said, Chass? The inspector doesn't believe that person in the red car even *exists*."

She walked to the door, picked up her bag, the one that we've had sitting by every front door of every house we've ever lived in.

"No, Mom," I said.

She turned and looked at me. "What did you say?"

"I said no. I've lived in like twenty-five towns in my life and I've had like twenty-five different names. No! Huh-uh! I like this place. I'm not leaving. This guy doesn't work for Kyle Van Epps. He's not going to kill us."

"What if he leaks your name to the press? What if they show your face on TV? Kyle Van Epps's goons will be here inside of two hours."

"Look, I figured out all that stuff that happened back in Alabama," I said. "I can figure this out too."

Mom looked at me for a long time. Finally she dropped her bag on the floor.

"One week," Mom said. "If you can solve this thing in one week, okay, fine. But if a week goes by and that jerk-off detective is still sniffing around you? Then we're out of here."

"Fine," I said.

"*Fine.*"

"I'm going to bed." I went in my room and slammed the door.

I lay on the bed for a while, staring at the ceiling. So

here I am, a sixteen-year-old kid and I'm going to solve a murder case with no clues and no suspects. A murder investigation where even the cops obviously don't know where to start. Yeah, right.

Great idea, Chass. Real great.

THREE

THE NEXT DAY I started getting calls from musicians who'd seen my posters. Mostly piano players, but some drummers and bass players too. So I started setting up auditions for my band.

I've been writing songs for a few years, but I only started playing in public in the past year. After we got to San Francisco, I went around to some coffeehouses and got a few gigs. One day this guy—he looked like he was in his early twenties, lots of tattoos and stuff—came up to me and said, "You really need to get involved in the real music scene."

"What?" I said. "This isn't *real* music I'm playing?"

"Nah nah nah," he said. "I don't mean that. There's kind of an underground scene around here. Real Music— that's what everybody calls it. It's not punk, it's not electronica, it's not alt country, it's not jam bands, it's not metal. But it's not this Britney Spears crap that everybody's listening to. It's just real music. But if you want to play in the Real Music scene, you need a band."

"I'm happy playing by myself," I said.

He looked around the coffeehouse where I was playing. There were about ten people sitting there, most of them reading or talking. Nobody had really been listening to me. "What's this place pay you?" he said.

"Fifty bucks," I said proudly.

He laughed like that was a pathetic joke, then he handed me a card. "My name's Justin Bates," he said. I read the card. It said REAL PRODUCTIONS—JUSTIN BATES, PRESIDENT. "I organize little get-togethers for the Real Music crowd. Kind of like raves, but without all that crap electronic music. I'm looking for quality musicians. You get a band together, a band that plays your songs, but with a little bit of a dance vibe to it—dude, I can get you a grand per gig."

I blinked. "You mean, like a *thousand* dollars?"

"Sure. You kick ass. You're hot. Your songs are great. All you need is a band."

"You're serious."

He flicked the card in my hand with his finger. "Get a band, dude. Then call me."

So that's what I was doing. I'd checked into this Real Music thing, and sure enough there were a fair number of places around the city where people playing music like mine were getting a big audience. Lately I felt like I'd heard Usher and Britney Spears till I was about to puke, so it was great to know that there were people out there who liked the same kind of thing I did. But Justin Bates was right. I needed a band.

What I did was I scheduled auditions. I felt kind of weird, this sixteen-year-old girl trying to audition professional musicians. But then at the same time I felt like, hey, why not? I didn't know much about life, but I knew one thing: I could sing. That had to be worth something.

Once I'd gotten enough calls from musicians, I set up a night where I could play in shifts of an hour apiece. I had met this guy who rented a room in a practice studio. It was like this huge warehouse that was divided up into tiny, plywood rooms that musicians could rent to use for practicing. This guy told me I could use his practice studio one night. There was already a drum kit and some amps, so all the musicians would have to do was walk in and plug in. That way I figured I could hear as many people in one night as possible.

I had sixteen people on the list. Ten keyboard players, two drummers, and three bass players and this girl who played flute. I figured I'd overlap the drummers and bass players and let the keyboard players each play for like half an hour. We'd go until I'd run through everybody. By then, hopefully, I'd have a band.

We started at six o'clock sharp. The first drummer was a fat, bald, middle-aged guy who told me about all these bands that he'd played with back in college, dropping names of all the supposedly famous musicians he'd played with—only I'd never heard of any of them. The first bass player was a skinny guy with lots of tattoos who looked at the floor and didn't talk much. The first keyboard player didn't show up.

So I played with the first two guys for a while. The drummer played really loud and kept going off on these big solos, and the bass player kept looking at the floor. He had a cooler full of beer that he kept next to his amp, and every time we finished a song, he would take a really long pull on his beer. Then the second keyboard player showed up. He was this annoying guy who kept calling me hon and trying to tell me how to sing, like, "Don't you think you ought to punch that line a little more, hon?" and stuff like that. At seven-forty-five, I said thanks, but he could go.

I played some more, and the bass player kept drinking beer. The third keyboard player showed up with a whole bunch of equipment. He had an old Hammond B3 organ and a Fender-Rhodes electric piano, and some other stuff, and he kept telling me about how this one was vintage such-and-such, and how this one had cost so many thousand dollars and been owned by some famous musician or whatever, and it took him about half an hour just to get set up. During which time the drummer alternated between playing really loud solos and talking about all the bands he'd been in. By now he was really sweaty from playing all these really loud solos. After a while he took his shirt off. He was real hairy and gross, with these big man-boobs. I felt like asking him if he wanted me to loan him a bra.

Finally the keyboard player with all the fancy vintage equipment finished setting up, and we played some more. After all that production, the keyboard player was TER-RIBLE! I mean he sucked *so* bad.

When I finally got rid of him, another old guy showed up and told me about how he'd been this musical prodigy when he was a kid, and while he was talking he stared at my chest a lot. He was actually pretty good, but he just had this pervy kind of attitude, and he gave me the creeps. We took a break, and he started telling me about how he had this great place up in the mountains and maybe I'd like to come skiing with him sometime.

I was like, "Dude, I'm sixteen."

And he goes, "Hey, I'm cool with that." I told him he could go, that somebody else needed to set up. He seemed kind of insulted.

Meanwhile the bass player kept drinking beer out of his cooler. About the time the second drummer showed up and I'd gotten rid of the sweaty, bald guy with the man-boobs, the bass player fell over on the floor, dead drunk.

I was starting to get really depressed.

The second drummer was a very sweet, nerdy little guy who hit the drums in this delicate, fearful way—like maybe he was afraid he might injure them. The next keyboard player was a high school kid about my age named TJ whose mother stood over in the corner and kept harassing him like, "You're missing the chords on the bridge, TJ! For godsake it's D minor, to G to Am, then four bars on C." The kid had really good technique, but he was so terrified of his mom that it was obvious he wasn't having any fun.

The next bass player showed up. He was about six foot three, a black guy, with an incredible physique and a face like a fashion model. We started playing, and he was totally amazing, the best musician I'd heard yet. He was doing all these cool things way up the neck of the bass, and finger popping and all these jazzy kind of lines and suddenly my music sounded ten times better than it ever had. At long last I was starting to get excited.

"Wow!" I said when we'd finished the first song. "You rock!"

"Hey, so do you, Sarah."

"Uh, it's Chass," I said. "My name's Chass."

He frowned. "You're not Sarah?"

"Chass."

"Oh," he said. "Damn. I must be in the wrong practice room. My bad."

He unplugged his bass and walked out of the room.

"Great," I said. "This is just great."

The next bass player finally showed up, the one who was actually *supposed* to be there. He had a shaved head, a swastika tattoo on the side of his neck, and pale skin like he'd just gotten out of prison. But at least he played okay.

The girl flute player showed up after that. She was probably five years older than me and she had about a million nose rings and cheek rings and ear rings and tummy rings and tribals, and her hair was dyed black. She rattled on about her yoga class and crystals and all kinds of weird New Age stuff and finally the bass player with the Nazi tattoos, went, "Hey. Pincushion. You play flute. How long does that take to set up? Pick up the pace, huh?"

The girl finally took out her flute, and we started playing again. She sounded like she'd started learning her instrument about ten minutes ago. She didn't even know what a chord or a key signature was. She was so bad, she didn't even seem to know she was bad, just tootling away with this happy, dopey look on her face.

When we were done with the first song, the bass player said, "Hey. Pincushion. Personally I pretty much hate the kind of music we're playing here. But this chick over here"—he pointed at me—"this chick *totally* sings her *ass* off. You should be embarrassed to even be in the same room as her. How about you pack up your flute and go take some lessons. Better yet, why don't you go home and kill yourself."

The flute girl started crying and ran out of the room.

The new keyboard player, a pudgy young guy in a Cal Poly T-shirt, said, "Hey, bro, that was not a very nice thing to say."

The Nazi bass player said, "If you don't take your finger out of my face, I'm gonna plant your ass in the ground."

"Okay, okay, okay," I said. "Let's take a break, huh?"

I went out to the drink machine and bought a Coke.

When I got back, the Nazi skinhead bass player was gone. The wimpy drummer said, "Gosh, he made me a little nervous."

"Yeah," the keyboard player said. "I know who he is. He used to be in this hard-core band back in the nineties. Then he got sent to prison."

"What for?" I said.

"Uh, I think he killed one of the other guys in his band."

The third bass player never showed up. A couple more keyboard players came and noodled around. They weren't bad, but I just didn't have any chemistry with them. Finally another guy came in and sat down on an amp. He was about my age, with a face so handsome it verged on being pretty. I did the math in my head. I was pretty sure all of the keyboard players had already played.

"Are you Don?" I said. "The bass player?"

He shook his head. We played one more song, and then everybody packed up and left. Except the really cute guy, who just kept sitting there.

"So," he said, when I'd gotten all the equipment turned off. "Any keepers?"

I sighed loudly. "I didn't realize getting a band together would be so hard."

He laughed really hard, and then suddenly his smile went away. "My name's Will," he said. "I'm Josh Emmit's little brother."

My eyes widened. I wasn't sure if I saw the resemblance or not. Where Josh Emmit had big, masculine features, Will was fine featured—almost as beautiful as a girl. "Oh my God, Will," I said. "I'm so sorry."

He nodded. "Thanks. Yeah. I'm still trying to get my mind around it. He was like my idol, you know. Now, boom, he's just gone. It doesn't even make sense."

I frowned. Obviously he wasn't here by accident.

"You're probably wondering why I'm here, huh?" he said.

I nodded.

"I was in the coffeehouse. I was supposed to meet Josh there. I saw you putting up the poster. So I just called your mom, and she told me you were here."

"Oh," I said.

"Look," he said, "I know you don't know me, but I'm here to ask for your help."

We walked out of the practice room and I locked the door. The plywood-lined hallway was a cacophony of music. There must have been twenty bands playing now—most of them death metal, it seemed like—guitars shrieking, drums thumping, all these guys singing like they'd just swallowed a bag of rocks. I motioned toward the door, and we walked outside. It was dark now and chilly.

"So how can I help you?" I said. I had this bad feeling that he was going to ask me about whatever it was that his brother had handed me. But then at the same time I was thinking—here's a golden opportunity to start my investigation.

Will looked around cautiously, like he was afraid someone would overhear us. Then, in a whisper, he said, "You ever hear of something called The Hundred?"

I decided to play dumb. "The Hundred? No."

"It's like a . . . club. Josh was a member."

"Okay."

"The thing that happened to him," Will said. "I think it had something to do with this group, this club."

"Like what?"

"You've never heard the rumors?"

"Not really."

He frowned at me for a moment, then said, "Well, it's real exclusive and social and all this stuff. But also, it's like it's—there's something real creepy about it. Some kids call it Club Dread. It's not just a club where people get together and goof around. It's like every year supposedly there's this game. It's kind of a role-playing thing . . ."

I made a face. "What—like Dungeons and Dragons or something. That doesn't sound very cool."

"Nah, nah. Deeper than that."

"What do you mean?"

Will shook his head. "I wish I knew. But I don't. Josh gave me some hints. He said he was into this thing. That he was trying to stop this thing that they were doing. Josh turns twenty-one this year, and when you turn twenty-one, you're automatically out. That's the rules of the group. But he wanted to stop whatever it was they were doing before he left."

I thought about what he was saying. As I was thinking, I was looking up and down the street. I noticed a Hummer sitting across the street from us. Someone was sitting inside, looking at us. I could tell it was a man, but I couldn't make out any details about his face.

"You mind if we walk?" I said. "I don't want to just stand here."

Will shrugged. "Sure."

We started walking. "Okay," I said. "So your brother wanted to stop this group, The Hundred, from doing something. What does that have to do with me?"

"Uh . . ." He paused.

"What?"

"Well . . . see I need somebody to infiltrate the group."

"*Infiltrate?*"

37

"Yeah. You know, sort of just sneak in."

Behind us I heard an engine crank up. I looked back. The Hummer had started up, its lights flicking on. As I watched, it pulled slowly into the deserted street.

"Sneak in?" I said. "How's that supposed to work? It's not like I'm exactly part of the social elite in this town."

"Nah, nah, nah, see that's the thing. It's not like just rich kids. The Hundred is for kids that just *got it going on*. Standouts. Musicians, athletes, models—I mean a really good surfer, a skate punk—they could be part of this thing. As long as they're cool. You'd be perfect. You're talented, you got a certain . . . vibe, you know. Plus you're kind of a honey."

"A honey. I don't think I've ever been called that in my life."

"Hey, I'm a honey connoisseur, dude," he said, suddenly cocky. "I would know. Anyway The Hundred, they're not looking for the head cheerleader type, getting ready to go to USC and pledge some little sorority, you know? That's too regular. What I'm saying, you're not like a *honey* honey. You're a little too weird for that."

"If that's your idea of a compliment . . ."

"Take it how you want it. All I'm saying, I'm sure you're the right material. Anyway, there's just one problem."

"Which is . . ."

"Well, The Hundred has these events. Parties, I guess you could call them. And the only way you can get in is to have a sort of pass. Everybody wears masks, so you're not identified by face. It's all about handing them your pass."

"Where do you get one?"

"Well, every member has one. I'm still trying to find Josh's, but when I do, I'll just give it to you. I'm gonna ransack his apartment tonight. There's a big event for The Hundred tomorrow night. It's where they initiate all the new members for the year. If I find the pass, will you go?"

I looked behind us again. The Hummer was back there, creeping along, its headlights playing against Will's pretty face. I was getting nervous.

"I don't suppose you know who's in that Hummer?"

He looked back. "That's just my manager."

"Your *manager*?"

The cocky look came back. He smiled a little at me. "Yeah, I've got a development deal with a record label. He's the guy who put it together."

"What's a development deal?"

"It's like where they invest a little money in you, trying to see if they think they can break you out big. The label hooks me up with a vocal coach, a choreographer, some big songwriters and producers—stuff like that. No big deal." From the way he said it, it was obvious he thought it *was* a big deal. And I guess it was. It didn't sound any fun to me, though. It sounded like a bunch of grown-ups trying to stuff some kid in a tight little box—turn him into a clone of his brother or Justin Timberlake or whoever—so they could make a bunch of money off of him.

But I didn't say that. Instead I looked at him curiously and then said, "Okay, so you want to infiltrate this group. Why don't you just do it yourself?"

"Because the way it works, there's a number on each pass. When each outgoing member passes the torch, they have to pass it to somebody of the opposite sex. Boys give it to girls, girls to boys. If I gave them Josh's pass, they'd compare the number, they'd see it had gone from boy to boy . . . and they'd know I wasn't legit."

I stood there in the moonlight and suddenly I felt cold. I shivered. "Here," Will said. "Take my coat." He draped it around me, and I could feel his warmth in the wool of the coat.

"Thanks."

"So," he said. "What do you think?"

I didn't say anything. I really wasn't sure if it was a good idea or not. It might give me a way to get Inspector Wise off my back. But then again, if he found out I was trying to join this group, The Hundred, it might just make him more suspicious of me.

"Look," he said, "you're a singer, right? Hey, I got a lot of connections in the industry. Do me a solid here, I could do you a lot of good."

I thought about it for a while. "What's this pass look like?" I said finally.

"It's like a little silver ingot about yay long." He held his fingers about four inches apart. "On one side it has a number carved or stamped into the silver."

My eyes widened. "I don't think you're going to find it at his apartment," I whispered.

Josh Emmit's brother frowned. "Why not?"

"Because I think he gave it to me yesterday."

"Excellent!" Will said. "Then it's a lock, huh?"

"Uh . . . ," I said. "There's a little problem."

After I explained the little problem, he offered me a ride back to my house. I was happy to accept. So I climbed into the yellow Hummer, and his manager drove me back to our apartment. When we got there, the manager hopped out and opened my door.

Will's manager was probably about forty years old, with a shaved head and a black leather jacket. He had very large shoulders, like he lifted weights, and funny little ears that looked like somebody had taken an iron and squashed them flat. Even though it was nighttime, he was wearing sunglasses, the wraparound kind that make you look like a cop who beats people up on the way to the police station. He smiled at me. "You have nice conversation with Will?" He had a thick Russian accent, one of those guys who never says *a* or *the*.

"Sure," I said.

"Good," he said. He pointed at my apartment. "Let me walk you up to your house."

"That's okay," I said.

"No, please," he said. "I'm old-fashioned guy. This neighborhood is not greatest. I would punish myself unmercifully, something happen to you, huh?"

"Okay," I said. I didn't like this guy, didn't like his smile or his sunglasses or his big weight-lifter neck.

We walked in the front entrance and up the stairs to the apartment where Mom and I live. I put the key in the lock.

"He wants you to play little detective game, am I right? Find out who killed Josh, whatnot?" Still with the big smile.

"Well . . . ," I said.

"Will is funny kid," he said. "Funny, funny kid."

I opened the door. "Thanks for walking me up," I said.

Without my inviting him in, he was suddenly inside

the room. "You mind if I use restroom?" he said. "I apologize, but I sit out there waiting on Will, drinking all that Starbucks, now I'm about to pop."

"Sure." I pointed to the door on the other side of the room. It's a small apartment, not much privacy. "Over there."

He went into the bathroom. It seemed like he was there for kind of a long time, the water running and running. When he came out he was still smiling his fake, slightly menacing smile. He walked over to me, and his smile broadened and he leaned forward, so that he barely had to whisper for me to hear him. "I want you to understand something, little girl. Will is *mine*. I *own* this boy. You get involved in his business, you're getting into mine. You see what I'm saying?"

"I'm not sure."

"So, I'm telling you, you don't want to get involved in my business." I could smell his breath, garlic and meat, whatever it was he'd had for supper. "Is hazardous to your health, you go mess around with my business."

"Hazardous to my *health*?"

He was still smiling. He put a large, strong hand on my shoulder, squeezed, his fingers digging right down to the bone until my eyes started to water. "You better believe, little girl. Your health, maybe your nice mom too."

I felt a sense of dread running through me. He mentioned my mom, but not my dad. How did he know I didn't have a father? It suggested to me that he had known things about me before Will had ever talked to me. Why would this guy even care about me?

"Okay, well thanks for that tip," I said. I tried to worm out of his grasp, but he was too strong for me.

He squeezed a little harder. When I was just about to scream, he finally let go. "Have nice day, little girl," he said. Then he patted me on the head, like I was five years old. He slipped out the door and was gone.

After he left, Mom came out in her bathrobe, looking half asleep. "Who was that?" she said sharply.

"Josh Emmit's brother's manager."

"What did he want?"

I started to tell her everything. But then I didn't. If I told her that this Russian guy knew enough about me to know that I didn't have a father, she would go from there to assume that he had been researching our backgrounds. In which case she would flip out and in ten minutes we'd be in the crappy old Volvo with our suitcases in the back, heading for another town.

"Chass?" Mom said. "What did he want?"

"Nothing," I said.

FOUR

THE NEXT DAY I was eating at the table over in the corner of the cafeteria where all the losers and geeks sat, when this kid came up to me and said, "You're Chass, right?"

I nodded. The boy was very short—not much taller than me, so maybe five foot five. He had short hair, moussed up into little points. The points were dyed blond, and the roots were almost black. His pants were baggy, his sneakers were fashionably torn, and he had this wiseass look on his face. "What's up?" I said.

He held up one of my blue posters. "You're looking for a keyboard player?"

"You play keys?"

"Among other things," he said, with a little smirk, like he was trying to make me think he was some kind of multi-instrumental prodigy.

I didn't really like the guy, just on first glance. He seemed like a typical short guy, overcompensating for being a shrimp. "So when we gonna hook up?" he said.

"I don't know . . . ," I said. "I was kind of looking for professionals."

"Oh! Really!" He lifted his eyebrows in an exaggerated way. "What, so pretty much you're too good for all us high school chumps?"

I shrugged.

He pointed at the hallway that led back toward the band room. "Nobody's using the practice room. You think you're hot, hey, bring it on. We can sneak back in there, I'll show you what real keyboard playing sounds like."

"I don't have my guitar."

"That's where the jazz band practices. They got every instrument in the world back there."

"I thought they were locked up."

He winked at me, dangled a set of keys in my face.

"You got a name?" I said.

"Marco," he said. "But you can call me Genius, if you want to. Or Mr. Fabulous. Or Your Eminence. Or—"

"I'll stick with Marco."

A few minutes later, we were set up in the practice room. "Play something," he said.

I started playing a song I'd written a while back. I wanted to show this cocky little jerk that I wasn't just some chick who strummed the guitar, so I played this really cool knuckle-buster of an intro, then started singing. For a minute he stared at me, expressionless. After a while he cracked his knuckles and stared at the ceiling. I couldn't even tell if he was listening.

When I was done, he looked at me with a sneaky smile on his face. "Damn," he said.

"What?"

"You know why I talked to you? 'Cause you're hot. I figured you'd suck. But, dude, I got to say, that wasn't too bad."

"Oh, thank you for that ringing endorsement."

"Who wrote the song?"

"I did."

He looked at me for a while, and then he said, "Play something else."

"I don't know," I said.

"Come on. Play something else."

So I did. He waited until the first chorus, then just kind of snuck into the song. He didn't ask me what key or what the chords were or anything. He was just totally *there,* boom. He was playing an electronic keyboard, getting this chunky vintage electric organ sound out of it. At first, he just played soft, sustained chords, but when the second chorus came around, he started playing a new line, a strange bass line that I never would have thought of, and he cranked up the volume a little. I couldn't even quite figure out what he did—but whatever it was, it gave a kick to the song, a shove, a push, something that knocked it over into a whole new place. On the third verse, he settled back into a soft groove—easy, not pushing too hard. Most musicians my age, if they have any skills, they play too much, showing you how great they can play. But not this kid. He just sat there in the pocket, backing me up, pushing me on, making me better.

I felt the hair come up on the back of my neck as I started into the chorus. He went charging back into the bass line he'd been doing earlier, pushing up the volume again. I pushed back, belting out the chorus at full volume, totally nailing it. I sang the last verse twice, then doubled the last line, my voice soaring.

When it was over, I just sat there for a minute, feeling the song wind its way out of me. I didn't like this kid much as a person. But, man, I had never felt a musical connection like that before. It just hit me, bam, like when you fall for a boy. Except different.

"Uh . . . ," I said.

"You felt it too," he said.

I shrugged. I didn't want to seem too eager. But at that moment, I would have torn off my left foot to keep playing with this kid.

"So that last song, Chass—you wrote that one too?"

"Yeah."

He just shook his head. "Aw, man, man, man . . ."

"What."

"I can't sing," he said. "I can't write. All I can do is play. So I've been waiting all my life for somebody as good as you to come along and take advantage of me." He flushed for a moment, then smirked. "Of my transcendent genius, I mean."

"So . . . are you playing with anybody else?" I said.

"I was."

"Meaning what?"

"Until three minutes ago I was playing in a couple different bands." He smiled. "But not anymore. The hell with those no-talent losers, dude. They can find another multi-instrumental genius. Now I'm in *your* band."

I didn't want to sound like I was letting him in my band just because he asked. But the truth was, there wasn't any question about it. He was *so* in.

"Cool," I said.

"Cool."

The bell rang.

"So," Marco said. "You want to hook up after school?"

"I've got something I need to do."

"I don't mean *hook up* hook up." He gave me this Slim Shady face. "I mean, you know, unless . . ."

"Let's stick to music." I thought about it for a minute. Last night I had told Josh Emmit's brother Will about throwing the ingot his brother had given me at the Dumpster, how it had missed and banked off into a pile of junk next to the Dumpster. Will had wanted to go look for it on the spot, but I had told him that was impossible, that I had to get home or Mom would kill me. I said I'd go find it the next day. "Maybe you could help me with this thing, Marco. Then when we get done, we could practice."

"Cool."

"Cool. See you after school."

FIVE

I WAS SUPPOSED to meet Marco at four on the corner near where Josh Emmit had been killed. Marco was late. It sort of gave me the creeps standing around by myself, just fifty feet from where Josh had died. There were three or four camera trucks still parked across the street, filming all these girls who were coming up and piling flowers and teddy bears and CDs on the sidewalk. For the past two days there had been practically nothing on TV but stuff about Josh Emmit getting shot. Marco showed up half an hour late accompanied by a light-skinned black guy, a little older than us. Maybe college age.

"I told you I'd make some calls," Marco said. "This is my boy Fabe. He's your new drummer."

"Hi, Fabe," I said. "Nothing personal, but you're my new drummer when *I* say you're my new drummer."

Fabe grinned. He was a very good-looking guy, with very even teeth, dreadlocks, a Stanford T-shirt, sunglasses, and about a million tattoos. He took off the sunglasses and his eyes were a strange green. "Hey, I can't control Shrimp's mouth. We'll jam a little, see if we're catching the same vibe or not. If not, no hard feelings."

"Dude, I told you, don't call me that," Marco said.

"Shrimp," I said. "I like that."

"Hey, kiss my ass."

I ignored him then pointed at an alley across the street. "See that Dumpster? I'm looking for a metal doodad, an ingot. It's like three or four inches long and has the number fifty-three carved into it. It should be on the ground next to the Dumpster."

Fabe looked curiously down the street, spotted all the teenyboppers dropping off flowers and stuff in front of Java Monkey. "Whoa," he said. "This is where Josh Emmit died, isn't it?"

I nodded.

He looked at the Dumpster. There was crime scene tape on the Dumpster too. "Wait a sec," he said. "Did you—" His eyes widened slightly. "Were you—"

I nodded. "Yeah. I was there when it happened."

"Okay . . ." He looked at me curiously for a minute. "So like whatever we're looking for—would I be correct in deducing that, say, it's some kind of evidence? Something related to the commission of a capital crime?"

"That's possible," I said.

"Then—just flesh this out for me—why are we not calling the police?"

"Frankly?" I said. "Because I'm a suspect. I'm trying to prove I had nothing to do with this."

Fabe looked at me for a long time, then turned to Marco. "You said she had awesome chops. You said she wrote great songs. That's all good. But what you failed to mention is that your little Nancy Drew friend here is totally whacked."

"Look," I said, "I didn't ask you to come here. I have to find something. That's just how it is. You can either help or not."

"I think I'll go with *not*." He smiled. "Nothing personal."

"Hey, I'll help," Marco said defensively. "You go sit over there next to that coffeehouse, Fabe, rest your delicate sensibilities while me and Chass go take care of business."

Fabe looked vaguely amused. "Whatever."

Marco and I walked across the street. "Despite all the tattoos, Fabe's a little bit of a Dudley Do-Right type," Marco said. "Totally sick drummer, though."

"We'll see," I said.

We reached the Dumpster, and I started trying to think back to the moment when I'd thrown the ingot away. "Let's try over there," I said, pointing at a stack of cardboard boxes. The boxes were full of rotting food from a restaurant next door.

"You know what?" Marco said. "Maybe I'll wander over there where Fabe is and just watch."

"Oh," I said, "you're one of those girly-type guys."

He stood up a little straighter. "Dude! I'm kidding." He started hauling the boxes out from the wall, dumping their contents in a heap. I grabbed a broken broom handle that lay on the ground and started poking through the stinking pile, looking for the ingot.

The day was fairly warm for San Francisco, and the warm air wafted the stink of the stuff up in our faces. "All I got to say is you better make me rich and famous," Marco said. "'Cause, man, you're gonna *owe* me."

I looked across the street. Fabe was sitting at a sidewalk table in front of a little restaurant, sipping on a cup of espresso in a tiny cup, his pinky finger sticking out in the air. He smiled and waved.

"If he wasn't such a great drummer," Marco said, "I'd go over there right now and cram that coffee cup down his throat."

"Let it go," I said. "Besides, I don't think you could pull it off."

"He doesn't look like it, but he's just a big sissy geek."

"As opposed to you . . ."

"As opposed to me, who's a master of Daito-ryu Aiki-jujitsu."

"What is that? Like, Japanese flower arranging?"

"Ha-ha."

Marco pulled three or four more boxes off the pile, threw them on the ground. I raked through them. "I don't know," I said. "I don't see it."

"Could it be back there?" He pointed deeper into the alleyway.

"Maybe." But it didn't seem right. I remembered hearing the clang of metal when the ingot hit the Dumpster. The way it was positioned, I didn't see how it could have bounced very far back into the alley.

But I followed him deeper into the alley anyway. He pulled out another box, threw it at the wall. It exploded, and a disgusting spray of rotten fruit flew all over the place.

"Hey!" The voice came from behind us, loud and accusing.

We whirled around. A guy in a chef's outfit stood in the doorway of the restaurant, holding a huge knife in his hands. "How many times have I told you little homeless retards to stop digging through the trash back here."

"We're not homeless," Marco said.

"I don't give a hoot what you are, pick this garbage up or I'm gonna serve you for supper." The chef waved his knife.

"Yo, bring it on, dude!" Marco said, picking up the broom handle and brandishing it in the air.

"Hey, hey, hey," I said quickly, stepping in front of Marco. "I'm really serious," I said. "I lost my, uh, my purse here the other day. I promise I'll pick everything up, but it's got a ring that my grandmother gave me, and my mom's gonna kill me if I don't find it."

The chef looked at me for a minute and then he seemed to calm down. "Well, I doubt it's here."

"Why?"

"I just chased some street kid out of here about half an hour ago. She picks up cans and wire and all this crap, sells it to a recycling place over on Allen Street. If it was here, she's probably got it by now."

"Damn it!" I said.

"What does she look like?" Marco said.

"I'm not talking to you," the chef said. Then he turned back to me. "Can't miss her. She's a Chinese girl, long hair. A street kid. Has a shopping cart with all this scrap metal in it. She goes up and down every street in this part of town, hunting through trash cans and Dumpsters. If she found your purse, I'm sure she'll sell whatever's in it."

"Fabe's got his ride," Marco said to me. "We could just cruise up and down the streets."

"Try the recycle place and those pawnshops on Allen, over on the other side of the one-oh-one. Like I say, if she found your purse, she'll head straight over there to sell the stuff in it."

"Thanks," I said. "I really appreciate it."

"Sure," the chef said. Then pointed his knife at Marco. "And you—you better not come around here shaking a stick at me, man, I'll take your head off."

"Keep talking, dude," Marco said.

"Hey! Hey!" I said.

Ten minutes later Fabe, Marco, and I were walking into a place that said ADOLPH'S SCRAP METAL on a rusty sign out front. It was on a bleak industrial street in the shadow of the 101, trucks thundering by over us.

"Hi," I said to the man at the counter. "I'm trying to find a Chinese girl who lives around here. I heard she brings in cans and stuff."

"A Chinese girl." The man at the counter had brown, horsey teeth and a cigarette dangling from his lip. He pointed down the street. "Sweetheart, Chinatown's about six blocks that way. I only see about eighty-five Chinese people a day in here."

"I was told she's a street person. Very young."

"You're talking about Annie. She's not Chinese."

"Oh?"

"Nah, she's Hmong."

"Mung?" I said it the way he pronounced it.

"*H-M-O-N-G.* Pronounced 'Mung.' They're like the hillbillies of Vietnam. Fought the Commies back in the war, then they all came over here after the war. She's Hmong."

"Okay, dude, so now we got all our Asian ethnicities cleared up," Marco said. "Has she come in here today?"

The guy behind the counter looked at me, then at Marco, then at me again. "I was getting along fine with you. But I'm not crazy about your shrimpy friend here."

"You call me shrimp again and I'm gonna—"

"He's a good organ player," I said. "Even if he is obnoxious."

"A good organ player?" The man behind the counter smiled his big horsey teeth at me. "Hey, shrimp, go play your organ someplace else, huh?"

Fabe took Marco's arm before he could start something and led him out of the store.

"Sorry about that," I said.

"Annie was in here a few hours ago," he said. "What do you need from her?"

"I dropped something," I said. "She may have found it. I'm thinking she might have tried to sell it. It's a little metal thing, like an ingot, silver, that has fifty-three stamped on one side and a hundred stamped on the other."

The man shrugged. "Nah. We don't buy stuff like that. Aluminum, copper, lead, steel—that's it. No precious metals. She sold me a car bumper once."

"Car bumper won't do it."

"Real silver?"

"Honestly I'm not sure."

"Silver trades at about five bucks an ounce. That'd be worth a couple hundred bucks easy. She'd probably try to move it at a pawnshop. There's one over on Richards Road that specializes in buying precious metals. Says 'We Buy Gold' on a sign outside. Guy that runs it is a shifty character, though. You say you *lost* it? See, here's the thing—if he's got the impression she stole it, he ain't gonna tell you he's got it. California law, pawnshops have to give up stolen merchandise, and they don't get any compensation."

"Okay, I'll bear that in mind."

The man took out his cigarette, set it gently on the counter with the lit part hanging off the edge. There was a row of little black scars along the whole length of the counter, like he'd been doing this for years. "So if he's the organ player, what are you?"

"I'm the singer."

"You can sing for me any day, hon." He showed me his brown teeth.

"Okay, yeah, thanks," I said. I left quickly.

"What'd he say? What'd he say?" Marco said.

"She came in, but she didn't have the ingot. There's a pawnshop around the corner that buys gold and stuff. He said she might try to pawn it there."

"So let's roll."

We started walking. "Tell me about yourself, Fabe," I said.

"Started playing drums when I was about five. I play in a jazz group that gigs around town. I've done some recording. I started Stanford this year, but I had to drop out after a semester. It was getting in the way of my gig-ging."

"No, it wasn't," Marco said. "You just wanted to piss your dad off."

Fabe made a noise like, *Pfffff*.

"His dad's some big lawyer out in the Valley," Marco said. "Works for all these high-tech companies. He wants Fabe to be just like him."

In a singsong Martin Luther King–sounding voice, Fabe went, "Son, I didn't go through all those sit-ins and freedom marches back in the sixties just so you could have the opportunity to be some degenerate musician. Boy, you got to *rise*. Boy, you got to *succeed*! Boy, you got to *overcome*!" He shook his head angrily. "I'm like, *dude, whatever*. The guy didn't go on any of those free-dom marches anyway. He was too busy memorizing tax loopholes."

We turned the corner, found ourselves on a street full of check-cashing stores and pawnshops—more of the signs in Korean and Chinese and Spanish than in English.

WE BUY GOLD, SILVER, PLATINUM one of them said.

I pointed. "There."

We walked into the shabby little place. Behind a counter in the back was an old Asian guy with a jeweler's loupe on his eye. In front of the counter was a girl about my age with long black hair. She didn't look homeless. She was fashionably dressed, clean, totally normal-looking. "Then give me my thing back, you asshole!" the girl was yelling.

"I'm telling you," the man said.

"And I'm telling *you*! Silver's five bucks an ounce. This thing's solid sterling silver. I want ninety-five bucks and I want my ax back."

The old guy behind the counter looked at her stone-faced. "Ninety-five, no way. Sixty. And no ax."

"Then give it back."

The old guy didn't move, just stared at her expressionlessly.

I walked back to them and said, "You know, I could probably clear this up."

The two of them looked at me like I'd just spit on them.

"Hey, sister," the girl said, "me and Mr. Leung are talking. Wait in line, huh?"

"The thing you're trying to pawn," I said. "It's mine."

"You don't even know what I'm doing here," she said.

"A silver ingot?" I said. "With some numbers stamped on it. You found it in an alley over where Josh Emmit got killed."

"I don't know what you're talking about."

I turned to the old guy. "You know the law, sir. If I tell the cops she stole it, then you have to give it back to me. And you don't get a nickel from the state. You want me to call the police right now?"

The old guy didn't say anything.

I held my hand toward Fabe. "May I borrow your cell phone?"

"All right, all right. Take it," the old guy said. He shoved something across the counter. A silver ingot.

The girl grabbed it before I could get to it. "It's mine," she said. "You know I didn't steal it."

"Look . . ." I said.

"Get out," the old man said, waving his hands. "All of you people, get out. You're disturbing my business."

"What business?" Marco said, looking around the empty room.

"Hey, I can call the cops just as easy as you," the old guy said. He held up a cell phone. "Out."

"I want my ax," the girl said.

"You give me a hundred twenty, I give you the ax," the pawnshop owner said. "You don't got the money, hey, get out of my shop."

"I need my ax."

She was pointing at something behind the counter. There was a long row of cheap guitars hanging from hooks. At the end of the row was a bass guitar.

I looked at Fabe. Fabe looked at Marco. Marco looked at me. Guitar players often used the word *ax* instead of *guitar*. "You got to be kidding me," Marco said.

"Do you play bass?" I said to the girl.

"Hey," she said. "Am I talking to you?" She turned back to the old guy. "I want my bass. I need to practice."

The old guy turned to me and said, "Every few days she comes in, pawns her bass. Then she comes back two, three days later, wants it back. What do I look like? A ministorage warehouse?"

"That bass is crap," Fabe said. "I got a nice Fender Precision back in my studio. Maybe we could make you a deal."

The girl whirled around. "A what?"

"A Fender Precision. Arguably the finest bass guitar on the planet."

"A Fender Precision for this ingot? Are you stupid or something? This ingot's worth maybe two hundred. A Fender's worth a grand, easy."

"I'm offering you a trade," Fabe said. "Take it or leave it."

"Where's your studio?"

"Out in the Valley."

"You drive me there? Take me back?"

"Sure."

She narrowed her eyes for a minute. "All right," she said finally. "But if you're thinking about ripping me off, don't. I'll mess you up."

"Do we look like a street gang?" Fabe said. "Please!"

The girl clicked her neatly manicured red fingernails on the counter for a moment, then shoved the ingot in her pocket.

"All right," she said. "Let's go."

Fabe had a very nice car, a BMW, parked on the street. Marco took the front seat. Annie and I climbed in the back, and off we went.

We drove for a while in silence and then Annie said, "So are you guys like a band or something?"

"Or something," I said.

"Well don't ask me to be in your band," she said. "Because I can tell just from looking at you that I'd hate your music."

"What makes you think we'd ask you to play with us anyway?" I said.

"For one thing? Because there aren't enough bass players in the world. Plus, let's face it, all guys are all like, 'Hey wouldn't it be cool to have a totally hot Asian chick in our band?' I'm sure that's why they invited *you*," she said to me. "'Hey, let's get the little blond honey— even if she can't play worth dick.'"

"Actually this is *my* band," I said hotly. "They just work for me."

Annie studied her perfect nails. "Whatever."

"Hey, I got an idea," Marco said. "Why don't you put a lid on all the hostility."

"Look who's talking," Fabe said, laughing.

We drove in silence out to Palo Alto, winding through expensive neighborhoods until we rolled up in front of a house that could only be described as palatial. Fabe parked his car next to a giant Mercedes.

"We have to go in the basement," Fabe said. "Dad won't let me come upstairs anymore."

"You're kidding," I said.

"For real. He stopped talking to me after I dropped out of school."

We got out of the car, walked around back past an enormous pool that was bigger than any house I'd ever lived in, then went inside.

"Holy crap!" Annie said. "This is your crib?"

Although there was a bed in the corner, it was no normal bedroom. Basically we were standing in a professional-quality studio control room—that happened to have a bed in it. Along one wall there were banks of faders, computer monitors, stacks of black boxes with knobs on them, huge speakers on the wall. Through a double-paned window we could see into a large studio, the walls lined with sound-deadening material, all kinds of instruments, microphones, and amps set up, including just about the largest drum set I'd ever seen in my life.

"Okay, Fabe," I said, "unless you really suck, you're totally in my band."

"Don't hate me just because I'm rich, talented, and amazingly attractive," he said. "I was just born that way." Then he pointed through the window. "There's your bass, Annie. How about you hand over the ingot."

"You're joking right?" she said. "Before I play it? It's probably broken."

"Can I just strangle this girl right now," Marco said. "I'm getting really sick of her."

"Go sit behind your keyboard," Fabe said.

We walked through a heavy door and into the studio. Annie walked over to a bass guitar that was leaning up against a huge amplifier. Her face suddenly softened. She reached out and touched it tentatively. "Wow. It's really beautiful." Then she picked it up, plugged a patch cord into the amp behind her. She thumped out a few deep notes, playing a little hip-hop riff.

"Okay, it works," Marco said, sitting down behind an electric piano. "You satisfied?"

Without any obvious thought, his hand snuck down to the power switch on his keyboard, flipped it on.

"I'm not sure I like the action," she said.

"You don't like the *action*," Marco said. "Good action, bad action, it's still worth five times as much as the ingot. For godsake, quit stalling."

Fabe sat on the throne behind the enormous drum set, picked up a stick, flipped it in the air a couple of times.

"So what kind of music do you like, Annie?" I said.

"Straight-up hard-core."

I looked at her perfect nails, her cute little sherbet-colored outfit, her nice little shoes. "You mean like hard-core *punk*," I said. "Where's your Mohawk? Where's the safety pin in your nose?"

"That has nothing to do with punk," she said. "Punk is about making your own rules. I'm in this band called Hot Shaved Asian Chicks. Maybe you've heard of us?"

We all looked at her blankly.

"Well, whatever. I'm sure Britney here is into some kind of tired-ass pop."

"That mike over there's hot, Chass," Fabe said to me. "Annie here's been so busy insulting you, maybe you ought to show her what you've got."

There was a row of guitars behind me—gorgeous Martins and Takamines and Gibsons. I picked up one of the Martins, strummed it. It was a little out of tune. I fiddled with it, plugged it into the PA system, played a few bars of the hardest knuckle-buster of a song I knew, then snuck a glance at Annie. She was making a big show of not being impressed.

"Sing that thing," Marco said to me. "The one we played at school." Then to Fabe he said, "Start out on the high hat, nice and soft. Let it build."

I played the intro to the song. Marco swiveled around to an old-fashioned electric organ that was set up next to the electric piano, started playing chords behind me, low and soft. Fabe kicked in as I started singing the verse, just riding the cymbals, barely doing anything at all. But it sounded perfect.

Annie looked at her nails, then looked at the ceiling as I sang. She wasn't quite rolling her eyes. But it was close.

"It's in G," Marco said to Annie after I'd sung the chorus. "Or is that outside the scope of your meager musical training?"

"Whatever," she said. Then she started playing, watching my fingers to catch the chord changes. She didn't do anything fancy, but it sounded nice. Fabe kicked it up a notch as I started singing the second verse, and Marco took the organ into another gear. I was starting to get the goose bump thing going again. Marco was right. Fabe was easily the best drummer I'd ever played with.

Annie stopped watching my fingers as Marco took a

short, tasty organ solo, then she closed her eyes, and started bobbing her head a little. She was doing something different now, something that had almost a hip-hop feel to it. It felt like it was punching the song up again. Fabe was playing harder now, sweat beading up on his forehead.

I sang the third verse. I had gotten used to singing it with just the guitar, but now that there was all this muscle behind the song, I sang it differently. It was a song about this guy that I used to know back in Alabama, that I was sort of in love with and how much it sucked when I had to leave him back there. The way I'd been singing it before, it was kind of like, *Oh, my life sucks, I'm so pathetic and whiny and everything*. But now it was like I was mad. And somehow that made the song better.

I just flat-out howled, just let it rip. And the band was building, building, building.

And then suddenly it was over and I could hear the ring of Fabe's cymbals fading away.

Marco was grinning. Fabe was looking at me with this funny expression on his face, like he hadn't really expected much out of me. Nobody made a sound for a long time.

Suddenly Annie took off the bass, pulled the ingot out of her pocket, and tossed it on the floor in front of me. "Okay," she said. "I guess I'll keep the bass. It doesn't suck all that bad. Who's gonna take me back down-town?"

"Oh, oh, oh!" Marco said. "Don't play me like that! You came all the way out here, you might as well jam with us a little bit."

"I told you, I play hard-core not this warmed-over John Mayer–type crap." She looked around. "Where's the case for my bass, dude?"

I scooped up the ingot.

"You are so full of it, Annie," Marco said. "You want to stay so bad you can taste it. Well, kiss my ass, we don't need you. Bass players are gonna be lined up around the block to play with her."

"I got stuff to do," she said.

"Like what?" Marco said. "Picking up more cans?"

Annie's face went hard as a rock.

I jumped in and said, "Aw, come on. One more song won't kill you."

Annie and Marco kept staring at each other for a while, eyes narrowed.

"I am *not* homeless, just for your information," she said finally. "Picking up cans happens to be a good way of making money. No jerky little boss, no time clock, no deep fat fryer. It's easy, and I can do it whenever I want."

"Who said anything about *homeless*?" Marco said. "Did I? No, I didn't."

"You were thinking it."

"One more song," I said.

"Just one more," Fabe said.

"If Shrimp here promises not to talk again until I leave."

Marco rolled his eyes. "Fine."

"Fine."

"Fine!"

Two hours later, we were still playing, when my cell phone rang. I answered, and a voice said, "Dude, it's Justin Bates, Real Productions. I gave you a business card a couple weeks ago?"

"Oh, hi," I said. It was the guy who'd given me the idea to start a band in the first place.

"So, look I heard that you hooked up with Fabe Daniels and that obnoxious little keyboard player Marco. Is that really true? Those guys are totally bad-ass."

"Yeah," I said. "In fact we're rehearsing right now."

"No kidding. So this band I booked for a thing I'm putting together this weekend broke up and I'm looking for a fill-in band. You think you could make it?"

"Uh, sure. I think."

"I could give you four hundred bucks."

"When we talked before you said like a thousand."

There was a long silence. "Did I say that? I don't think I said that. Maybe I could go five."

"Let me ask the guys," I said. "See what our availability's looking like."

"Okay, okay, six hundred. But that's as far as I can go."

"I'll call you right back, okay?"

I hung up the phone. "So y'all want a gig on Friday?" I said.

Marco and Fabe looked at each other.

"Sure," Marco said.

"Sure," Fabe said.

"You want to play with us?" I said to Annie.

"Hey, I'm just jamming cause Spoiled Rich Boy here won't get out from behind his drum set and drive me home," she said. "I only play hard-core."

"You'll make a hundred and fifty bucks," I said.

"What time do we go on?" She didn't even crack a smile.

SIX

AN HOUR LATER I was doing homework in my living room.

My phone rang. "Hey, Chass." It was a boy's voice. "It's Will. So did you manage to find the ingot?"

"Yeah."

"Thank God. I just found out that this party for The Hundred—it's tonight."

"What? I've got a test in algebra two tomorrow."

"A test! Come on! We're talking about people murdering my brother here!"

74

"Look, I don't know, I've got the ingot. Maybe I could just give it to you and you could find somebody else."

There was a long silence.

"Did Mikhail say something to you?"

"Mikhail?"

"My manager. I saw him talking to you when he let you out of the car. Was he telling you not to get involved?"

"Sort of."

"Awwww man. Look. That guy, he thinks he's like Joe Russian Mobster. But he's not. It's just a big front. He wouldn't hurt a flea."

"He sure hurt my shoulder last night."

"Hey, I'll talk to him about that. I promise, he won't lay a finger on you."

I thought about it. "My mom's not gonna be happy. I really do have a test."

"Fifty years from now, what are you gonna remember about this night? How you got a B minus on some math test because you didn't study? Or how you helped put a murderer behind bars and started yourself down the path to being a huge star?"

"Okay, you're laying it on a little thick," I said.

He laughed. "I'll pick you up at nine-thirty."

"Wait," I said. "Mom won't even let me stay out past ten on a school night. I'll—"

But the phone was dead.

"Dammit," I said.

"Who was that?" Mom said. "And don't swear in the house."

"It was Josh Emmit's brother. He wants me to do something tonight. I'll have to stay out late."

"Don't you have an algebra test tomorrow?"

"I've got study hall fourth period," I said. "I'll be ready."

"It's a school night."

"Mom!" I said. "A guy got murdered here!"

"I don't care. It's a school night."

"Fifty years from now, who's going to remember I only made a B, uh, I mean an A minus—on some math test? Versus finding out who killed Josh Emmit?"

Mom sighed. "Okay, I'm making a huge exception here. But keep your cell phone on. And if you get home one minute past midnight, you are in big big big trouble, young lady."

SEVEN

"ARE YOU SURE we're in the right place?" I said.

Will Emmit had just stopped at the curb in the middle of a down-at-the-heels warehouse district in a part of town I'd never been to. There was an elevated freeway nearby, maybe the 101, with traffic zooming by. The place we were next to looked like a warehouse or abandoned factory—scarred red brick, surrounded by a rusted chain-link fence. A couple of very large black guys in hooded sweatshirts loitered on the corner.

"Those guys are security," Will said. "Just go down

there and show them the ingot. They'll tell you what to do." He turned and looked at me. "Where's your mask?"

I held up a cheap plastic Catwoman mask that I'd bought at a 99-cent store near my house.

"Not exactly original," he said.

"That's the point."

"Okay," he said, "here's what you need to be looking for. Before he died, Josh had said to me that he thought the group was getting out of control. And he wanted to stop it. He believed that somebody had found out."

"I'll see what I can find out," I said.

"So can you find a way to get yourself home? I need to get going."

"Sure," I said.

Will started to go then said, "Oh and another thing to keep your eye out for. If anybody mentions anything about some missing music, some missing masters, that could have something to do with it too."

"Missing music?"

He waved his hand. "Hey, it's probably nothing. Just keep your ears open."

I approached the two guys standing on the corner, feeling like a fool with my kid's Catwoman mask on. I noticed both men wore small chin microphones and had little receivers in their ears. They looked up and down the road, like they were trying to see if anybody was watching.

"What you got?" one said.

I showed them the ingot.

"Turn around," the other one said. "Spread your arms." He frisked me. It was creepy, this stranger running his hands all up and down my body. There didn't seem to be anything personal about it, but he touched me everywhere. I mean, *everywhere*. Then he ran a black electronic wand up and down my body, sort of like the things they use in airports.

"All right, you're good," he said. Then he put his finger up to his earpiece and said, "Number Fifty-three arriving." Then he opened a gate in the chain-link fence. Painted on the blacktop were two purple stripes that glowed slightly in the light of the dim streetlamp. "Follow the stripes, Number Fifty-three," he said. "Don't go outside them."

As I walked slowly down the blacktop, I had this sort of paranoid feeling. Like, what if this whole thing is some kind of big joke that's being played on me? Like, I'm going to get to the end of this line and there won't be a party. I'll just get killed or something and then my body will get stuffed in an oil drum and that'll be the end of me.

I followed the glowing purple stripes around a corner,

found myself between two buildings. Both of them were lightless, empty looking. I stopped dead and stood there. I felt like I couldn't even move. I don't know why I felt so scared, but for a minute I just felt like turning around and running away.

I stopped dead. After a minute I heard footsteps moving toward me from the direction I'd come. Slow, tentative heel clicks, like someone was trying to sneak up on me. Still I couldn't move.

Suddenly, out of the blackness, a figure appeared. The figure, barely visible in the dark, screamed. Then the light shifted, and I made out a face. It was a girl about my own age, wearing a small, black Lone Ranger mask.

"Oh, my God!" she said, laughing nervously. "What are you doing? You scared the crap out of me!"

"No, you scared me," I said. "I was about to turn around and haul ass."

She started laughing. "Sorry, this is my first time," she said. "I'm a little nervous."

"Me too," I said.

She stepped toward me, and now I could see her better. She was a tall girl, all Goth-ed out in black, with stiletto heels and a perfect flat stomach and long perfect legs showing. "I guess we're not supposed to say our names," she said. "I'm Number Seventeen."

"Fifty-three," I said.

"Cool. Let's go."

We walked together for another hundred yards or so, winding past big empty steel containers and rusted machinery until the purple stripes came up to a door. Another ominous-looking black guy stood by the door.

"Initiates do not mingle with members," he said. "Initiates do not speak unless spoken to. Initiates follow the purple stripes. One foot outside the stripes, you will be escorted off the premises and your ingot confiscated. Clear?"

We both nodded.

We showed him our ingots, and without speaking, he opened a heavy steel door next to him. As soon as the door opened, loud electronic dance music spilled out. The bass was so loud I could feel it in my chest. It was dance music but full of threatening-sounding clanks and weird, dissonant instruments and strange voices whispering things that you couldn't make out.

We entered a huge black-painted room. There were a lot of kids dancing. They all wore masks. Most of them were just black, Lone Ranger–type masks like Number 17 was wearing, but some of them were elaborate and obviously handmade, while a couple were just cheap plastic Halloween masks like the one I wore. Some kids wore formal clothes, others dressed like they were out clubbing, while others, like me, were dressed just like they always dressed. What I noticed about them was they all moved with confidence, that they were all attractive. There were no fat kids, no spazzes, nobody leaning against the wall and looking at the floor. The cool factor was off the charts. I felt totally out of place, like they'd be on to me in a second. No way I'd fit in with all these hypercool people.

The kids all ignored us, though, as Number 17 and I followed the purple stripes through the large room. We then left the room and walked down a small corridor— the music fading as we walked. Eventually we entered a small, ugly room painted a drab green. It looked like a lunchroom cafeteria from a really old, really run-down school.

Kneeling on the floor on the far side of the room were about fifteen kids, their heads covered by black bags. Everybody was fit, well built, dressed in really unusual or interesting ways.

"Kneel." I turned and saw a tall girl, a few years older than me, standing by the door. She reminded me of Angelina Jolie—big lips, big boobs, mean expression. She was pointing at the end of the line. Seventeen and I walked over and knelt. The tall girl approached us and placed a black cloth bag over my head. It cut out all light, tickled my face.

"Okay, all of the initiates are here," she said. "From

here on out you will never use your own name, only the number on your ingot. Do not move. Do not talk. You will be summoned."

In the distance I could hear the spooky dance music. I don't know how long I stayed there on my knees. Long enough that it started to really hurt. After a while, the music stopped. It was now totally silent. I could hear my own breathing. It was starting to get really hot in the hood.

"This sucks," somebody said after a while. A boy.

"Number Seventy-nine, stand up." It was the mean girl talking, the one with the Angelina Jolie lips. "Place your ingot on the floor, follow the purple stripes out to the front door. You have failed to follow instructions."

"What! I was just—"

"Now. Or somebody big and ugly will drag you out."

"This is total BS," the boy said sullenly. But his footsteps went out the door, disappeared down the hallway.

We waited for a while. My knees were starting to kill me.

Just when I felt like I couldn't stand it anymore, I heard something in the distance, a shout. Somebody shouted back. I couldn't make out the words. The shouting went back and forth—not like they were angry, but like they were chanting something. It started getting louder. Then there were more and more voices, chanting something deep and inarticulate. I don't know why, but I'd never felt so scared in my life. I was literally shaking.

"Up!" It was the mean girl.

I could hear us all standing up, everybody grunting and sighing as the blood started flowing back into their knees.

"Hold your right hand out in front of you."

I did as I was told. I could feel someone take my hand, place it on the shoulder of the person next to me— Number 17, the Goth chick I'd seen outside. I guess the mean girl was lining everybody up, each person holding the shoulder of the person next to them.

"Walk," she said. "Follow the person whose shoulder you're holding."

We staggered forward, holding on for dear life, trying not to bang into anything as we walked blindly out the door and down the hallway toward the chanting.

Eventually the chanting surrounded us. I still couldn't make out what they were saying. There were words, but it was like they were in some foreign language that I'd never heard before. We kept stumbling slowly forward, trying not to trip. Eventually Number 17 stopped, so I stopped too.

The chanting got louder and louder and louder. Just when I felt like I was about to pee in my pants, the chanting abruptly ended.

The room was silent.

Finally a voice called out, "Kneel, Initiates!" It was a girl's voice, but not the mean girl who looked like Angelina Jolie. This was somebody else.

We all did as we were told, knelt again on our sore knees.

"You have been chosen," the girl's voice said.

"YOU ARE THE SELECT!" echoed the entire chorus of kids in the room.

"Our secrets are our own."

"SWORN TO DEATH."

"Life is the game."

"PLAY THE GAME."

"We are The Hundred."

"PLAY THE GAME."

"Take off your hoods, Initiates. Then turn around."

I took off my hood. Arranged around us in a semicircle were all the kids in the group. The room was dark, and it was hard to make out their faces. As instructed, I turned. Standing on a plywood stage in the bright cone of a spotlight were two people, a boy and a girl.

They were both dressed in black. Not Goth or anything, just wearing black clothes. The boy wore black jeans, cowboy boots, a black T-shirt, and a black leather jacket. He was buff, but not in a pumped-up-jock sort of way. The girl wore a black evening dress that showed every curve of her body. Her skin was very pale, and her hair was so blond it almost looked dyed. But you could tell it wasn't.

"So, look," the boy said. He had a soft voice, not so quiet you couldn't hear it, but soft enough you had to listen hard. There was something about it, though, that made you want to listen to what he had to say. "This is it. The Hundred. Each year, we play a game. One winner. One loser. Everybody else has fun. The winner of the game gets something good, something they really want. The loser, well . . ." He shrugged. "The loser is the loser. What can I say. Everybody in this room hates losers. Right?"

There was a chorus of agreement from the room.

"The Hundred is all about the game," he said. "In the game, there are no rules. There's no right or wrong. There are no lies and no truth. There's just the game."

"Actually there's one rule," echoed the girl on the platform.

"Yeah, okay, one rule," the boy said.

"No one talks," the girl said.

"NO ONE TALKS." The whole room came back like an echo.

"No one talks," he repeated. "Say it, Initiates."

I felt the words coming out of my throat like I was breathing dust. "No one talks," I said.

"This is *our* thing," the boy said. "It's not for our

parents. It's not for our buddies. It's not for the cops. It's not for anybody but us. We are The Hundred."

"WE ARE THE HUNDRED."

"No one talks."

"NO ONE TALKS."

"Our motto . . ."

"OUR MOTTO . . ."

"Trust no one!"

"TRUST NO ONE!"

The room was silent for a long time. The boy and the girl on the stage were looking down at us, studying us. I could feel my heart hammering in my chest. I felt kind of sick, and I wasn't quite sure why.

"Any questions before you get initiated?" the boy said.

One kid held up his hand.

"You don't have to hold up your hand. This isn't school."

"Yeah, okay, sorry I uh—"

"And don't apologize. The Hundred is not about apologies. The Hundred is about winning."

"Okay, sure. Um. I'm still, I don't quite understand what this is all about. What's the game?"

"You'll find out what the game is after you become initiated. But I will tell you this—this isn't some kind of Dungeons and Dragons crap where you're the all-powerful gizmo wizard for a while and then you're not. In The Hundred, you don't play the game. You *are* the game. No going back. You can't be like, *Oh, gosh, Mommy, Daddy, I didn't realize what I was getting into, I'm all scared, I'm all*—No. Huh-uh. Dude, either you get ready to bring it on, or you stand up and get the hell out of here. Is that clear enough for you?"

The kid who had asked the question stared back at him. Finally he stood up, turned, walked out of the room.

"Good," the boy on the stage said, pleasantly. "Good for you. It's good to have your priorities straight." He paused, waited for the sound of the door banging shut behind the boy who had just left. "You soft, nauseating little sissy."

Everybody laughed.

I realized, suddenly, why I felt so creeped out by these people. It wasn't the chanting, it wasn't the weird music, it wasn't the huge dark room or the scary security guys outside. It was that I didn't like these kids. They all seemed like they were sizing you up, figuring out how they could use you. I don't want to use the word *evil*. But it was something close to that. It was like their eyes were all dead and cold, like they hated everything and everybody.

"Initiates," the girl on the stage said. "Are you ready to join us?"

"Yeah," I said. Everyone else mumbled along with me.

"Please speak loudly and clearly," the boy said softly. "The whole point of this group is you gotta learn to sound like you mean it." He grinned brightly. "Even when you don't."

"Initiates, are you ready to play the game?"

"Yes," I said loudly.

The boy pointed at me. "Did you hear her? How nice and loud and serious she sounded? Number Fifty-three there has a ghost of a chance of being a winner here. Whereas most of you, frankly, sound like candidates to be this year's big loser."

"Initiates, are you ready to join The Hundred?"

"Yes!" I said. Even louder this time. We were all louder now, like a bunch of marines at boot camp or something.

"Will you go running home to Mommy and give up our secrets?"

"No!"

"Do you understand that really, really, really, intensely bad stuff will happen to you if you break your word?"

"Yes!"

The boy and girl on the stage looked at us for a long time. Finally, they turned to each other, shrugged, then looked out at the crowd.

"Losers," one of the kids in the crowd said.

"Losers!" somebody else yelled.

"Losers, losers!" They started closing in around us, chanting, "Losers! Losers! Losers!"

I could see their eyes glinting behind their masks. Their faces were twisted with anger, hatred, spite. They pressed in and in on us, jostling us, shoving us, pinching us, poking us. And all around us the chant.

"LOSERS. LOSERS. LOSERS. LOSERS."

For a minute I thought maybe they would actually attack us, but then the shoving and pinching and poking stopped, and the anger and spite seemed to abate and they were just kind of rocking back and forth, all of them staring at us with cold, dead eyes, and the chant took on an almost musical sound, washing over us in slow waves. "LOSERS LOSERS LOSERS . . ."

I don't know why, but that seemed even worse than the anger. Now it was almost like we weren't even human to them. I imagined that this might just go on forever and ever, like some kind of bad dream where you get stuck in some terrible place and you can't get free. I could feel my hands shaking, my heart beating fast, sweat running down my neck. I was doing everything I could not to panic and run out of there.

I just kept thinking about the music that afternoon, how great it had been. I knew that if I stayed here, I had a chance of finding out what happened to Josh Emmit. I could feel it, Josh Emmit's murder somehow floating in the air around me. If I got up and left, a week would go by and the cops would still be asking me questions and I'd be no closer to a solution. And at the end of the week, Mom would tell me to pack my suitcase and go. And I'd never reclaim the feeling I'd had playing that afternoon with Marco and Fabe and Annie. Never.

About the time I was feeling like I couldn't stand being there anymore, I heard a loud wail. Down at the end of the row of initiates, one of the kids stood up and ripped his mask off. His eyes were wide, and he was totally flipping out, screaming something I couldn't understand. Hands grabbed him, and a bunch of kids hustled him out the door. And like that, the room was silent.

Suddenly everyone burst into smiles.

"All right!" the boy on stage called out.

"That's it," the girl said. "As soon as one kid flips out, it's over. Welcome to The Hundred."

"Stand up!"

We stood there in a line, and every one of the kids in the room filed by us and gave us a big hug. "Welcome," they'd say. Or, "Good job!" Or, "Way to go." Or, "Nice, dude. Very nice."

And they all seemed really sincere. And for a minute I felt this glow of comradeship and belonging, like I had just found a family. But then finally, the girl and the boy on the stage were the last ones to hug us. The girl put her arms around me and hugged me close. I got this weird feeling, like I was being hugged by a guy. Her fingernails kind of slid inside the tail of my shirt, raking softly across the small of my back. I felt her lips on my ear and her hot breath. For a second I thought maybe she was kissing me. But then she just whispered, "I'm Twenty-four. Trust no one."

I felt all the warmth drain out of me.

The boy from the stage was last. He put his arms around me, and there was something just really sexy about him. At the same time, he scared the crap out of me—though I can't say exactly why. He whispered to me, "I'm Ninety-six. Be careful with Twenty-Four. She's a total lesbo." I thought maybe he'd let go, but he didn't. After a second I sort of tried to get away from him, but he said, "I know all about Josh Emmit. You weren't his choice. You aren't supposed to be here. I can't prove it. But I'm going to make it my first job to get you out of here."

Chills ran up my back. I didn't know what to say. Then, suddenly, it came to me. "Liar," I said softly.

He laughed, stepped back, a big grin on his face. "I like you, Fifty-three. I like you a whole lot."

Then he and the girl went back up on the stage. "Congratulations, losers," the girl said, pleasantly. "You're in The Hundred now. In a little while, we'll announce how this year's game is going to work."

The music started immediately, and a lot of the kids started dancing. I sort of slunk off to the side and watched. Okay, so I was here. Now what? It wasn't like I could just go around asking people if they'd killed Josh Emmit.

I talked to a few people, brought up the subject of Josh Emmit's murder—but the music was so loud you could hardly talk to anybody anyway, and nobody seemed to be all that interested. It was like they were all too cool to be interested in Josh Emmit.

It was getting later and later. About 11:40 I figured I needed to get going.

Just then the music went off again and the lights went down, and the spotlight came up on the makeshift stage at the far end of the room. The guy dressed in black and the pale girl with the blond hair were standing there again.

"Okay, guys," the girl called out. "The moment you've all been waiting for."

"The game," the boy said.

"For those of you who are new to our happy little group," the girl said, "let me tell you more about the game. Every year, the game is different. The one thing in common is that one person loses, and one person wins.

What does the winner get? The answer is, whatever they want."

"Let me back up," the boy said. "For those of you who don't know, The Hundred has been around for a long, long time. We don't even know how old it is, but it goes back at least to the beginning of the twentieth century. Maybe longer. We don't keep records, we don't write things down. Stuff just gets lost in the mist."

"What we do know, is that the brightest, most ambitious, most gifted kids in this city have been playing this game for a long time. That means that there are former members of The Hundred in every field in the world. You want to be a movie star? There's an ex-member of The Hundred out there who can make it happen. Want to get into Harvard? Want to dance on Broadway? Want to work for a senator? Doesn't matter. There's somebody out there who can make it happen."

"And all you have to do . . ." The boy in black looked around the room.

The girl smiled thinly. ". . . is win."

"The late lamented Josh Emmit? He was a winner five years ago, when he was just sixteen years old. Very impressive performance. You think a no-talent jerk like Josh Emmit would have become famous without help? Not likely. But that's what happens when you're a winner."

"This year," the girl chimed in, "we have a particularly nasty game."

"It's called The Chump Did It."

"And how, one may ask, does one play The Chump Did It?"

The girl and boy were doing a little routine, like they were hosts on some lame TV show. "I'll tell you how you play, Number Twenty-four."

"Please do, Number Ninety-six!"

"Thanks, Twenty-four, I will. The answer is, you win the game by framing another member of the group by making it look like they committed a crime they didn't commit."

The pale blond looked around at all the other kids. "And before you think about stuffing a dime bag of weed in some kid's locker, sorry dude, that won't hack it. It has to be a real crime."

"As you all know, our little group has a coordinating committee called The Ten. The Ten will act as a jury. If somebody gets framed, the crime goes before The Ten. If we decide the crime is too lame, too obvious, too gay . . ."

". . . then you're automatically out of the running."

"That means you better go for something good," Ninety-six said. "Like armed robbery would be cool."

"Or art theft."

Somebody in the audience said, "Is anything off limits?"

"Murder?" another kid said.

The two kids on the stage looked at each other, then at the group. They smiled. "Murder? Dude, that would be . . ." The girl looked at the boy.

The boy grinned. ". . . totally exceptional. Total slam dunk."

I looked at my watch. It was very close to midnight. I was going to be late for sure. Mom was going to kill me. Plus, I had had way too much of these horrible kids.

"One last thing," the girl said. "This year we've added a little twist."

"This year, there's a time limit."

"We're having a party this coming weekend. Saturday night. The winner will be announced at the end of the party."

I had heard all I needed to hear. I turned and headed toward the exit. As I got close to the door, a tall red-haired girl near the door detached herself from a conversation with a boy and came over in my direction. She brushed by me and, without looking at me, said, "Meet me outside in about five minutes. We need to talk."

"Do I know you?" I said.

"Five minutes," she said. Then she was gone.

EIGHT

FIVE MINUTES LATER, on the nose, the tall red-haired girl came out the front gate of the warehouse property. The two imposing security guards were still standing there. We walked silently down the empty street. When we were out of sight of the building, she took off her mask. I recognized her then as a kid from my high school, a senior. Her name was Clarissa Echols. She was the president of the student council and had the lead role in the school play and all that stuff. Supposedly she was going to Yale to study acting in the fall. She was green-eyed and attractive, but a little high-strung looking, like she was always worried about something.

"Okay?" I said.

"Look, you can take your mask off," Clarissa Echols said. "I know who you are."

I didn't take the mask off though.

"You're Chass," she said.

I shrugged.

"Look, here's the thing, Chass. I know you weren't Josh's pick."

"Oh yeah?"

"It doesn't matter to me. But some of the people in The Hundred—they're kind of nuts. If they find out for sure that you weren't Josh's pick, they're gonna wonder how you got the ingot. And what you're doing here."

"So let them wonder," I said.

"Look, most of these kids in The Hundred, it's just a social thing. They don't take it seriously. But the core group—Ingrid and Neil and some of the others."

"Who are Ingrid and Neil?"

"Ingrid Leonard and Neil Ostrov. The two kids who made all the announcements."

"I thought we weren't supposed to know anybody's names. I thought it was all anonymous."

Clarissa shrugged. "Nobody pays attention to any of that crap."

"Then why would they care if I was or wasn't Josh's real pick?"

"Because the core group—Ingrid and Neil and some others, they're into some really scary stuff. I mean you heard them. Framing somebody for *murder*? That's crazy."

"If it's all so crazy, then why are you here?"

She looked around furtively. "Once you're in, it's hard to get out."

"Well, I'm in already, aren't I?"

"It's different with you. Nobody knows you yet. You haven't . . . gotten involved."

"Gotten involved how?"

"There's more to this group than it seems like. There's the parties. That's why most of the kids are here. There's the game. Some people are into that. And then there's . . ."

"There's what?"

She hesitated. "Other stuff. Look, there's a reason why kids call this Club Dread. Anyway it doesn't matter."

I studied Clarissa's face. She looked very sincere. Sincere and scared. Of course, that was part of the whole act in The Hundred, wasn't it—acting sincere when you were actually lying? "Does any of this have to do with Josh's murder?" I said.

Clarissa sighed. "That's kind of my point. I don't

know who killed Josh, and I don't want to. If you weren't Josh's real pick, you had to get hold of the ingot somehow. And you have to be here for a reason. Somebody is going to start going, 'Hmm, maybe she's just here to snoop around.' And if they do . . ." Clarissa Echols looked off into the night.

"If they do, what?"

"You could end up like Josh."

"You really think some kids murdered him? Kids from The Hundred?"

"Maybe."

"So how do you know all this stuff? I don't understand why some huge star like him would bother with some silly group like this."

"Most kids quit once they go off to college, they drop out of the group. But Josh never went to college. He was already a pop star before he got out of high school. When he was working hard, making records or touring or whatever, he'd kind of drop out of The Hundred. But sometimes between tours or whatever, he'd have a lot of time on his hands and just sort of drift back into the group. Plus, he and Neil have been best friends since they were kids. Whatever Neil's into, Josh's into."

"How do you know all this stuff?"

Clarissa didn't answer for a minute. "Josh is my brother," she said finally.

I frowned. "You don't look much alike."

"He's my half brother actually. My mom left his dad when he was real young."

"What about Will? Is he your brother too?"

"Will?"

"You know, Josh's brother Will."

She looked at me quizzically. "Josh doesn't have a brother," she said finally.

"I must have made a mistake," I said. I turned and started walking away from her. I could feel her eyes burning into my back.

NINE

THE NEXT DAY we had an assembly instead of class during first period. I spotted Marco slumped down in a seat near the back of the auditorium.

"What's up?" he said. We rapped knuckles, and I sat down next to him.

"I hate assemblies," I said. "What are we getting today—Officer Friendly telling us to just say no?"

"Nah," Marco said. "Student council elections. A bunch of morons giving speeches about how we need more school spirit."

"Great," I said.

The assembly started, and the principal, Dr. Litwin, introduced this eager-beaver-looking kid named Dwayne Chin, who was apparently the vice president of the student council. He started talking about how vital student council elections were and how every vote counted and all that crap.

"Where's Clarissa Echols?" I whispered. "Doesn't the student council president usually lead this sort of assembly?"

"You didn't hear?" Marco said.

"What?"

"Yeah, she had a nervous breakdown or something. These guys in white coats came to her house this morning, and they had to take her away in a truck, screaming her head off."

A boy sitting next to Marco leaned over and whispered, "No, dude, I heard it was drug rehab. She didn't want to go, but her parents made her. They put her in handcuffs."

A girl in front of us turned around and whispered. "You guys are so *mean*. None of that stuff's true. This girl on the bus this morning lives next door to her? And she said what it was, she had food poisoning and this ambulance came and took her away."

"Dude!" the boy next to Marco said, "it was totally

drugs. My friend on the wrestling team, Yung-gook Kim, he knows Clarissa's sister's best friend. Everybody knows she's a total dope fiend."

"I heard she was a narc," the girl said.

The principal suddenly stood up and walked to the microphone. "Excuse me, Dwayne," he said. "I hate to interrupt, but you people need to settle down back there." He pointed directly at me and Marco. "If you don't extend Dwayne the courtesy of listening in silence, then you'll have a few days detention hall to reflect on how rude you're being."

"Rehab," the boy next to Marco whispered.

"Nervous breakdown, dude," Marco whispered.

"Food poisoning," the girl whispered.

Marco threw a piece of wadded-up paper at the back of her head. It bounced off her head and fell in my lap.

"Settle *down*!" Dr. Litwin shouted.

I was feeling scared all of a sudden. Not because of Dr. Litwin, but because I felt sure that whatever had happened to Clarissa Echols must have had something to do with her conversation with me. Or at least it was an awful big coincidence.

One of the teachers in the back of the auditorium came up and snatched the piece of wadded-up paper off my lap. "You want to tell me about this?" she said.

"What," I said. "I didn't do anything."

TEN

AFTER SCHOOL I got together with the band at Fabe's studio, and we started working on some cover songs so that we'd have enough material to play for our gig on Friday night. I was used to just learning a song and playing it however I felt like. But with a whole band, you had to work out how you were going to do the intro, how many times you'd repeat the last chorus and all this stuff. It was a lot more work than I expected. Annie and Marco kept getting mad at each other, blaming each other for screwups and that sort of thing.

Annie and Marco were going at each other for about the tenth time when my cell phone rang.

"Hello?"

"Hey, it's Will."

I didn't say anything. I really wasn't even sure what to say, now that I'd found out he had lied to me.

"You there?" Will said.

"Yeah. What do you need?"

"Look, can we get together?" he said. "There's been a development."

I clicked my fingernails on the top of my guitar for a moment, thinking. If Will was lying about being Josh's brother, there was no telling what else he'd lied about. For all I knew, *he* could have shot Josh. "Is it something we can do on the phone?"

"I'd rather do it in person," he said.

I agreed to meet him at a coffeehouse down in the Mission District. After I got off the phone, I told everybody about this guy Will, how he claimed to be Josh's brother but wasn't.

"We should come with you," Fabe said.

"Nah, nah," I said. "That's okay."

"Come *on*!" Annie said. "We're your straight-up homies now, girl. We got your back." She tapped her chest just over her heart with her fist, then pointed a couple of fingers at me like some gangster off the TV.

"She's right," Marco said. "You're rollin' with a posse now."

Annie looked at him with hard eyes. "Are you making fun of me?"

Marco looked insulted. "No, dude! I'm just saying."

She kept looking at him for a minute, then finally said, "All *right* then."

"All right then," Marco said.

We arrived at the coffeehouse off Van Ness at around seven. The yellow Hummer was parked across the street, and I could see Will's Russian manager—if that's what he really was—sitting in the front seat with his sunglasses on. We went inside the coffeehouse and Will was sitting there at a table, waiting.

He grinned at me then looked around at Fabe, Marco, and Annie. "What's up with the crew?" he said. "I was hoping we could kind of be private about this."

"This is my band," I said. "They know everything."

"For instance," Fabe said, "we know Josh Emmit doesn't have a brother."

"Look, uh . . ." Will flushed and sort of stared at the ground.

"Go on," I said. "I'm real eager to hear this. Like, for instance, what's your last name?"

Will flushed. "My name's Will Gaffney. I've known

Josh for a long time. He's not my brother, but he's *like* my brother. I just told you that because I'm desperate. Everything else I told you was true. I have a development deal with the same record company as Josh. Josh had volunteered to sing on the CD I'm making. In fact, he went out on a limb for me, got this real big producer to work with me on it. It was a big, *big* track, dude. I mean this was gonna be my hit. With him singing on it and everything? Man . . ."

"So what's the problem?"

"Okay, here's the thing. Josh got into a dispute with his record company. About money, I think. So the record company said that until it was resolved, they owned the masters and Josh couldn't touch them."

"Wait," I said, "I don't understand that."

"When you record a CD," Fabe chimed in, "all the music is on the hard drive of a computer. That's your master. You can't produce a CD that you can sell without a master. So basically if the record company says, 'Okay we're keeping the master,' then you're screwed. You've got no record."

"Right," Will said. "That's exactly what happened. I mean it was months and months and months of hard work. Needless to say Josh was pissed. So he snuck into the studio where it was recorded, downloaded all the tracks, and erased the hard drive."

"I still don't see the problem."

"The day after he downloaded all the tracks, they disappeared."

"You mean *his* copy," Annie said. "The one *he* downloaded."

"Right. Somebody stole them. And the day after that, he's dead."

"I still don't see what this has to do with you lying to me," I said.

"Look, it was *his* producer who did my track, the one that's gonna make me blow up. And when Josh was downloading all his tracks, guess what else he downloaded?"

"Your song."

Will nodded. "I have to find it. I mean, somebody stole it from Josh, right? Whoever killed him is probably who stole it."

"Okay . . ."

"Josh and this guy, this friend of his, had recently had a big fight. I'm not sure what about, but that's not important. Point is, I think this friend of his stole the master. I think he may have killed Josh too—though I'm not sure about that."

"You're talking about a guy named Neil, right?" I said.

Will nodded. "Neil Ostrov. Really slippery character. He's some kind of honcho in this group, The Hundred.

So I figured if I could get you into The Hundred, get you next to him, maybe you could help me figure out where my master is."

"That still doesn't explain why you lied."

He shrugged. "I just . . . you know I figured you'd buy the sympathy angle if I said I was his brother. Whereas if I said I wanted you to do something dangerous so that I could get rich and famous—well, you'd have probably thought I was an asshole and told me to buzz off."

"That's kind of how I'm feeling right now," I said. "Didn't it occur to you that eventually I was going to find out?"

Will didn't answer for a minute. Finally, he said, "Look, here we are. All I can do is apologize. I feel like a total jerk and I'm sorry. But I can't change what I did. Bottom line here, are you in or out?"

I looked around at the guys in my band, spread my hands like, *What should I do?*

"To hell with him," Annie said. "He's a liar."

"I agree," Marco said.

"Look!" Annie said, raising one eyebrow at me. "The shrimp actually agrees with me." He punched her in the arm. She punched him back.

"Ow!" Marco said.

I looked at Fabe. "Look at the big picture," he said. "According to what you've told us, this cop suspects you of shooting Josh. You still need this thing to get solved. Probably a lot more than Will does. The fact that Will lied to you doesn't change that."

I thought about it for a minute. "Yep," I said finally. "Fabe's right. I don't particularly trust you anymore. But I'm still in." I folded my arms skeptically, leaned back in my chair. "So what have you got for me?"

Will leaned over, opened up a manila folder. "Couple of things. First, I can't tell you how I got this, but I've got a copy of the autopsy report and some of the investigation files." He set the folder on the table. "I don't know what this will do for you, but I'll summarize what I found."

"Okay."

"The autopsy says cause of death was a gunshot wound. No surprise there. He was shot twice, once in the chest and once in the stomach. The ballistics report says he was shot with some kind of weird pistol called a Toka . . . Toka . . . uh . . ."

"A Tokarev," Marco said. "It's a Russian pistol."

"Right. Tokarev. I guess they can tell that from the bullets somehow."

"How'd you know that?" Annie said to Marco.

Marco shrugged. "I'm a competition pistol shooter. I know a lot of stuff about weapons."

"Anyway," Will said, "that's not the main reason I

wanted to meet with you. The main thing is this." He reached into his pocket, pulled out a tiny electronic device about the size of a cell phone.

"What is it?" I said.

"It's a digital audio recorder. It records onto a chip instead of a tape. Josh carried it around all the time. If a song idea came to him, he'd just sing it in here."

"So what's on it?" I said.

"Press PLAY."

I did.

A tinny voice came out of the recorder. "Dude, what are you talking about?"

"That's Josh," Will said. "The next voice you hear will be Neil Ostrov's."

"I'm not trying to be a dick about this," Neil's voice said from the recorder. "But it's time to pay up, son."

"Pay up what?"

There was a long pause. "Come on," Neil said finally. "You know what I'm talking about."

"Spell it out for me."

"Sixty-three thousand bucks."

"Neil, bro, you know I'm good for it. I'm just in a jam right now. This whole contract thing with the record company is hitting my cash flow kind of hard."

"Look, that's not my problem."

"Neil, you're my friend!"

"And I'm trying to help you, Josh. It's just—dude, sixty-three grand! This has gotten too big for me. This is out of my hands."

"What, are you saying that some Italian guy is gonna come put a dead horse's head in my bed? Or break my legs?"

"Not an Italian guy, no."

Again there was a long silence. "You're serious. You're saying somebody's gonna hurt me. Who the hell are you mixed up with, Neil?"

"What, you think I do this on my own? Obviously I've got somebody backing me. And it's not freaking the Bank of America."

"Oh, man. Oh, man. This sucks, Neil."

"I know it does. But I'm just telling you. The guys I'm dealing with, they're telling me you've got twenty-four hours to come up with some cash."

"Or else what?"

"You know what, dude. You *know* what."

"Cut me some slack, Neil! There's got to be something."

There was a sound of something rustling around. Then Neil said, "Actually . . ."

"Actually what?"

"They might be willing to work something out."

"Like what?"

"Like this master that you got? Maybe if you signed some papers, signed over the master to these guys . . ."

"Out of the question!"

"Then you need the cash by close of business tomorrow."

Will reached out and turned off the recorder. "That's the end of it," he said. "But it's obvious that Neil was involved in something bad here."

"Drugs?" Fabe said. "Was he selling stuff to Josh?"

"Josh wasn't into that," Will said.

"Then what?"

"I don't know," Will said. "I was hoping you might be able to find out."

"How would I do that?"

"I heard The Hundred is having another party this weekend. It's not like an official party, it's just that some of the people are showing up."

"No masks or anything?" I said.

"Nah. It's kind of like a rave. Have you heard of this scene, the Real Music thing?"

"Sure," I said.

"Well, there's this dude I know named Justin Bates who puts together these parties. He's doing one on Friday night. Supposedly all these kids from The Hundred will be there."

"You're kidding," I said.

Will frowned. "What?"

Fabe started laughing. "Dude, we're the band."

"I know you're a band—"

"No, we're *the* band," I said. "For Justin Bates's rave thing."

Will started to laugh. "Sweet! Then all you got to do is get next to Neil, start pumping him about Josh."

"I don't think Neil likes me."

Will looked at me for a second then laughed. "I promise you, Neil likes you. You're exactly his type."

"What type is that?"

"The female type," Will said.

Everybody laughed.

"All right then," Will said. "I got to scoot."

As we stood up, Annie stuck her finger in Will's face. "Hey. Listen up. You lied to my girl about Josh Emmit's brother. Don't be lying to her again. Or else I'ma take a baseball bat upside your head. Huh? Okay? Huh?"

"Yeah," Marco said. "Me too."

Will laughed, pointed at Marco. "Listen to the shrimp here! He's like her sidekick."

We watched him walk out the door, get into the yellow Hummer with his Russian manager at the wheel.

"*Side*kick," Marco said. "I'm gonna put a sidekick up his—"

"Let it go," I said. "Let it go."

ELEVEN

I WAS AWAKENED early the next morning by the sound of loud banging. It took me a minute to realize what it was: someone pounding on the door. I stumbled out of my room in my pajamas in time to see Mom answer the door, leaving the chain on, and looking out through the crack.

"It's Inspector Wise, SFPD," a loud voice said. "Open up."

Mom looked back at me with a slightly panicky expression on her face, then she undid the chain. Three men and a woman, all of them with badges hanging off their belts, walked into the room. Inspector Wise was in front, carrying a piece of pale blue paper in his hand. He handed it to Mom.

"Search warrant, ma'am," he said. "You and the girl have a seat on the couch."

Mom sat next to me.

"Can they do this?" I said.

Mom didn't answer. She was reading the paper that the inspector had given her. "I think they can," she said finally.

I looked over her shoulder. It said SEARCH WAR-RANT at the top with a bunch of legal-sounding stuff underneath. There was a judge's signature on it, and a seal pressed into the paper. As I was reading, the police detectives had pulled on blue surgical gloves and fanned out into the apartment, opening the kitchen cabinets, the closet doors, the drawers of our furniture.

"They won't find anything," I said. I could see the female detective in my room, going through my underwear drawer. "You're not gonna find anything!" I yelled.

The female detective turned and looked at me with a hard, empty expression. "Darling, take my advice, keep your trap shut."

"Unless you have something important you want to get off your chest," Inspector Wise said.

I crossed my arms and sank down into the couch. In my room I could see the hard-faced woman pulling out my clothes, piling them on my bed. All my underwear, my socks, my bras. Then she was opening a box of tampons, lining the tampons up on the bed. I felt so embarrassed. Embarrassed and angry.

After about half an hour, the woman came out of my room, shook her head.

"Come on," the inspector said. "You haven't been there for fifteen minutes."

"I've never seen anything like it," the detective said. "These people have got no personal belongings."

A second detective came out of Mom's bedroom. "No photos, no old phone bills, no cancelled checks, no love notes, no nothing."

"We lost everything in a fire," Mom said.

"Nothing in the kitchen, either," the third detective said.

The inspector ignored her. "Who got the bathroom?" the inspector said.

"I thought you did," the female detective said.

"I thought *she* had it," the detective from Mom's bedroom said.

"Get the bathroom, Ray," the inspector said.

The detective who had been in the kitchen walked into the bathroom, closed the door. There was some thumping and bumping around. After about ten minutes he came back out and shook his head.

Inspector Wise's eyes narrowed slightly. "You sure?"

The detective, a youngish guy with a kind of dopey expression on his face, shook his head. "I checked everything."

"All right." Inspector Wise took out a piece of paper on a clipboard and said, "Okay, I'll need you to sign this form saying that we have not taken any property from your home."

"How would I know?" Mom said. "You could have snuck off with a pair of my underpants."

Inspector Wise sighed loudly. "You gonna sign or not?"

"Go in your room, Chass," Mom said. "Check and make sure everything's there. These people wasted our time, now let's return the favor."

I went back in my room. One of the detectives went into the bathroom. After a minute I heard the toilet flush. I went back out and said, "It's all there." I just wanted the cops to leave. The whole thing just felt icky and disgusting. I didn't like having these people in all my private things, poking around in my underclothes, messing around in my bathroom.

Mom seemed to be in no rush, though. Finally she came out and said, "Okay, it's all there."

"Then sign the paper."

The female detective came out of the bathroom, wiping her hands on her pants. "There are towels in there," Mom said. "Feel free to use them."

"Are you gonna sign or not?"

"Let me see that search warrant first," Mom said. She took the blue paper and read over it. "It says here that your warrant is based on information from a confidential informant. Who is this person?"

Inspector Wise smiled humorlessly. "Well, now, they wouldn't be confidential if I told you, would they?"

Please please please please please just let them get out of here, I was thinking. I could hear the toilet running.

"I think you just made this up," Mom said. "You have absolutely nothing on my daughter."

"You want to lodge a complaint?" the inspector said. "Hey, I'll give you the number for the departmental complaint line. It's 1-800-BITE-ME."

"Oh, good. A humorist," Mom said.

"Sign the paper, lady, or don't. I don't care."

Mom took the clipboard, signed it, handed it back to him. I could still hear the toilet running and running.

The cops all walked to the door, started to leave. Inspector Wise stopped and said, "Your toilet's running, ma'am. You ought to call your landlord, get that fixed."

Mom looked at him stonily.

Then the inspector's eyes narrowed. He turned and yelled down the stairway. "Hey! Ray! Did you check inside the toilet tank?"

I couldn't hear what the answer was, but suddenly the inspector looked angry. "That moron," he said. Then he charged back into the bathroom, pulled the lid off the water tank on the back of the toilet. He looked at me, winked, and grinned. "That was very, very close, hon." He took off his jacket, then rolled up his sleeve. I couldn't figure out what he was doing. Then he reached into the water, pulled something out, and held it up to me.

It was a plastic bag, with something black inside. I couldn't tell what it was from where I was standing. But I could feel my heart sinking in my chest. Suddenly I wanted to throw up.

"By golly," the inspector said cheerfully. "What have we here? Why I believe it's a Tokarev pistol. Nine millimeter, if I'm not mistaken."

TWELVE

HALF AN HOUR later, I was back in the little room down at the police station again. Mom and I sat next to each other on one side of the stainless steel table.

"I don't know how that gun got there," I said after the inspector left the room. "I swear to God."

"They have microphones in the room," Mom said. "They're listening to us right this minute. Do not speak another word until our lawyer gets here."

We sat in silence for a really long time. Finally an

older guy with a long gray ponytail and a really expensive-looking blue suit came in and sat down.

"Hi, Tom," Mom said.

The guy named Tom shook her hand. "How are you?" he said. "Good to see you again."

"This is your lawyer, Chass. His name's Tom Steele. He's one of the top criminal lawyers in San Francisco."

"*The* top." Tom Steele smiled at me. But the way he smiled it was more like he was smiling at himself than at me. There was something about him I didn't like. He reminded me of an actor, Tom Cruise or somebody like that, who needed to have people looking at him all the time, telling him how great he was.

"Is anybody listening to us?" Mom said.

"As long as I'm here, no," the lawyer said. "If they did, I'd have this case thrown out in a heartbeat." He paused. "So. What's happened here?"

Mom gave him a thumbnail sketch of my situation.

The lawyer took notes on a pad of yellow paper. When Mom was through talking, he said, "First, I'm going to advise you not to say anything else to the police. Whether you're guilty or innocent, every word you speak can come back to haunt you later."

"But I didn't do anything."

"I understand that's your position, but—"

"My *position*? I'm telling you somebody planted that gun."

He gave me his I'm-so-great smile. "And I'm just saying, guilty or innocent, at this point it's not in your interest to talk."

"Okay."

"That said, what I'd like to do is bring the inspector back in here and let him think I'm going to let you talk. What I want to do is to force him to give up as much of his case as possible in hopes of provoking a confession."

I shrugged. "Whatever."

"But this requires that you absolutely, absolutely keep your mouth shut. Okay? Can you stick with the program?"

I didn't like his condescending manner. But I didn't really know what else to do. I looked at Mom.

"I think you should do what he says," she said.

"Okay."

The lawyer stood up briskly, buttoned his jacket, walked out.

After a few minutes he came back with Inspector Wise. Wise sat down opposite us, set a file on the table. I could see him looking nervously at my lawyer, like he was a little intimidated by him.

"Okay," Tom Steele said. "My client wants to do

everything she can to help, and to straighten out this misunderstanding. If you're willing to sit down with us and go through what you've got, she'll do what she can to help clear up your questions."

"I think I can work with that," the inspector said. Then he turned to me. "Look, I understand there may be other people involved. If you can show me how you were forced to do something against your will, or tell me about other people who might have been involved in the death of Josh Emmit, now's the time to get it on the table. Then maybe we can work with you, keep this in the juvenile system. That way you won't have to serve time in an adult prison."

"But I didn't do anything!"

Tom Steele put his hand on my arm. I closed my mouth.

"Jerry," Tom Steele said to the detective. "Explain to us where you're coming from. We'll try to help."

"What's your full name?" Inspector Wise said to me.

"No, no, no, no," Tom Steele said. "It doesn't work that way. If you want to turn on the hot lights and start asking her questions, then we're done here."

"Just because you're some hotshot lawyer, you think I'm just going to sit here and lay out my whole case, huh?" the inspector said.

"No. I think you'll do it because, if you want any

questions answered by my client, you don't have any choice."

The inspector thought about it for a minute, then finally said, "All right, let's start with the gun. Forensic evidence shows that Josh Emmit was shot with a Tokarev nine-millimeter pistol. Same model as the one we fished out of her toilet."

"Okay, what else?" Tom Steele said.

"By her own admission, your client was at the scene of the crime. By her own admission she was speaking to Josh Emmit when he was shot. We have a witness who places a shiny object in her hand."

"Mm-hm." The lawyer wrote something on his pad. "Keep going."

"I want to know how she explains that."

"We'll get to her explanation later," the lawyer said, not looking up. Now that he was putting his condescending attitude to work for me, I was starting to like him a lot better. "Keep talking."

Inspector Wise took out a photo, set it in front of me. "You recognize this gentleman?"

"Sure," I said. It was Will's manager. "That's—"

"Nuh! Nuh! Hup! Whoa!" the lawyer held his hand in front of my face. "No talking, Chass. We're in the listening phase of this conversation."

"This man," the inspector said, "goes by the name

Mike Peters. Real name Mikhail Petrovich. He's Ukranian. Wrestled for the Soviet Union in the 1980 Olympics, got a bronze medal. Later served five years in Soviet prison for assault. He's been linked to the Ukranian mob. Very bad guy."

"That's fascinating," Tom Steele said. "The fact that my client was talking to him means nothing. What does this guy do for a living now?"

"He pretends he manages musical acts. But that's just a front for a bunch of things. Loan sharking, credit card scams, gambling."

"What's loan sharking?" I said.

"Sh!" my lawyer said.

"It's loaning money for very high rates of interest," the inspector said. "It's illegal."

The inspector took away the photograph. "When we first spoke, you pretended that you had no knowledge of a group called The Hundred. Correct?"

I didn't say anything.

"Well," he went on, "we had a meeting of this group under surveillance last week. Guess who I saw walking in?"

"Tell us," the lawyer said.

The inspector put a photo on the table. It showed me in my Catwoman mask.

"It looks like a girl in a Catwoman mask," the lawyer said.

"To me it looks like Chass," the inspector said.

The lawyer frowned, stared, shook his head. "Nah. Uh-uh. Don't see the resemblance." He looked up and smiled. "But do go on, I'm very interested."

"So how much do you know about your innocent-looking clients here?" the inspector said.

"I take it that's a rhetorical question, Jerry?" Tom Steele said.

"Well, I'll tell you what I've found out," Inspector Wise said. "Let's start with the young lady. She says her real name is Clarissa Barber, but everyone calls her Chass. How strange. It's especially strange, because when I called the folks at the high school in Quincy, Ohio, where she claims to have lived last—guess what? They've never heard of her."

"Go on."

"So what about Mom, here?" the inspector said. "Ms. Deirdre Barber. No record of anybody in Quincy, Ohio, by the name Deirdre Barber. No phone records, no cell records, no nothing. So I check a little further, run her through all the databases. Guess what? Deirdre Barber doesn't exist."

"And this is a crime?" Tom Steele said. "People running from domestic abuse change their identities all the time."

"Is that what your situation is?" the inspector said to Mom. "You're on the run from a crazed ex-husband, something like that?"

"Talk to *me*, Jerry," the lawyer said. When the inspector looked grudgingly back at him, he continued, "And I'm not saying that's their situation. But I'm not saying it's not either. Anyway, before you got into that, you brought up something called The Hundred. What does that have to do with Josh Emmit?"

"Frankly, we're not sure," Inspector Wise said. "We know that he was a member of a secretive youth group called The Hundred. Sometimes called Club Dread. I can't give you specifics, but there may be a connection between his murder and the group."

"Okay, so what else have you got that we could explain for you?"

"For now, that's all."

My lawyer reached across the table and grabbed the investigation file before Inspector Wise had a chance to take it. He flipped through it slowly, then eventually closed it.

"So basically," Tom Steele said, "what you think at this point is that my client came into town a couple of months ago, and after no contact with Josh Emmit in her entire life, runs into him on the street, pulls a gun on him, and shoots him. That's just ridiculous on the face of it."

"Then why did she have the murder weapon in her toilet?"

"You have yet to establish that it's the murder weapon."

"Okay. So we'll run the ballistics. What are the odds she had a Tokarev innocently taped to the inside of her john?"

"Let me ask you a better question," my lawyer said. "I just looked at the autopsy report. You allege that my client was standing right next to Josh Emmit when she shot him. How come there's no stippling?"

"Excuse me?"

"Come on. You read the autopsy report. You know as well as I do that when you shoot a gun at somebody at a close range, particles of burning gunpowder are expelled from the barrel of the gun. If the shot is fired at a close range—under six feet, let's say—those particles fly into the skin of the victim, leaving a bunch of little black dots tattooed or burned into the skin around the wound. It's called stippling. Show me the stippling."

Tom Steele flipped a photograph out onto the table. It was a close-up of a red hole in a very white patch of skin. I gasped. Sickening as the picture was, I had to look. There were no little black dots on the skin around the wound.

"He was wearing a shirt," Inspector Wise said dismissively. "You don't usually get tattooing of the skin when the victim's wearing a shirt."

"Then there should be stippling on the shirt." Steele flipped through the pictures until he found a bloody T-shirt. "Here it is. Show me the burns. Show me the stippling."

Inspector Wise glanced at the picture, flushed for a moment, then grabbed the file and stuck all the pictures inside.

"The shooter was in the red car, Inspector," my lawyer said. "You know it and I know it."

"This proves nothing."

"You're so confident? Arrest my client."

The room was silent for a long time. "We're gonna run the ballistics on that gun, Tom. If there's a match to the bullets that killed this kid, I'm charging your client with murder."

"So until then, I guess she's free to go, huh?"

Wise glared. "You said she was going to answer my questions."

My lawyer sighed theatrically. "Well, gosh, Inspector, that was my plan. But now that I've evaluated the situation, I really can't allow my client to talk any further until we've had a chance to consult." He turned to me and Mom. "Ladies, let's go."

"You can consult right now," Inspector Wise said.

"I don't think so." Tom Steele gave the inspector his condescending smile.

"This whole situation smells," the inspector said. "It's going to take me about two days to get the results back on those bullets." He stuck his finger in my face. "Then you're going down, sweetie."

When we left the room, I could barely walk, my legs were trembling so hard. We followed Tom Steele down the hallway and out the front door of the station. When we had reached the street, he stopped and said, "Look, Chass. I have to be honest with you. If that gun comes back a positive match for the bullets they took out of Josh Emmit's chest, you're going to have a hard time beating this thing. Is there anything you want to tell me, anything I can work with? If there's somebody else involved in this, particularly an adult, we might be able to unload this whole thing on them."

"How many times do I have to say it," I shouted. "I didn't do it."

"Keep your voice down," my lawyer said.

Mom's face hardened. "If my daughter says she didn't do it, then she didn't do it."

"Look," I said. "That guy they showed in the picture. The Ukranian guy? He came up the other day and used my bathroom. I remember it seemed like he was in there for a long time. He must have planted it then."

Tom Steele ran his hand through his graying hair. "All right," he said dubiously. "That's a start. But there's got to be more to this. If we're going to beat this thing, we've got to put somebody in the car that you saw. The inspector claims that nobody saw the car. Nobody but you."

"I know," I said. "I know."

THIRTEEN

AS WE DROVE away from the police station, I said to Mom, "Can I ask you something, Mom?"

"Sure." Mom looked kind of distracted.

"It was obvious that you and Mr. Steele knew each other already."

"Uh-huh."

"I mean if he's really the top criminal lawyer in San Francisco, like he said, then wouldn't he cost a lot of money?"

Mom didn't answer.

"We don't have much money, Mom. How can you afford to pay him?"

She sighed. "Look, honey," she said finally. "There are some things I haven't told you."

"Like what?"

"You and I have been running since you were little. As you know, the reason we started running was that I had information about Kyle Van Epps. Information about how he killed somebody a long time ago."

"Sure."

"Well, there's more to it. Some things I've never told you. After we'd been running for a few years, I decided to fight back. As you know, Kyle Van Epps is head of Apex Global Media, a company that owns a variety of smaller companies. When you were little I had gotten a job—more or less by accident—at a company that was owned by Apex. While I was there I found some things that they were doing that were illegal. I didn't think anything of it at the time. But then after we'd moved on to another town, I started wondering if what they were doing was being done throughout Apex. So I got a part-time job in the accounting department of another part of the company. I found more irregularities. It's all real boring stuff. Accounting. But what it comes down to is that Kyle Van Epps has been stealing from his company for a long time. And I've been investigating it. Putting together the information."

"What does that have to do with that lawyer, Mr. Steele?"

"Well, I was getting very close to having all the information I needed to convict Kyle Van Epps back when we were in Alabama. But I wasn't quite there. In order to make the final connection, I was going to have to get very close to these . . . irregularities. And to do that, there was a danger that I'd have to do some things that weren't . . . strictly legal. So when we moved here, I got in contact with Tom Steele. He's been working with me ever since."

"How are you paying him?"

Mom looked uncomfortable. "I'd rather not get into that."

"Okay," I said. "Do you trust him?"

She shrugged. "As much as I trust anybody, I guess."

"Because I didn't like him."

"I can't say he's my favorite person, either. But you don't become a successful criminal lawyer unless you're good at keeping secrets."

I nodded.

"But I don't care how good a lawyer he is," she said. "I'm not comfortable with where this whole thing is going. I'm terrified that we're going to wake up tomorrow and your face is going to be on the news. If that happens, Kyle Van Epps will know right where we are. And he'll come for us."

I didn't want to leave. I didn't want to leave Marco and Fabe and Annie. I didn't want to leave my music. Leaving Alabama, where I had last lived, had sucked so bad. I just didn't want to go through it again. New school, new friends, new apartment, new name, new everything. I tried to think of something that would change Mom's mind.

"Look," I said. "Inspector Wise said it would take two days to run the ballistics. This weekend there's a big shindig for this group, The Hundred. I have a hunch I know who killed Josh. I think I can use this party to prove he's the killer."

Mom studied my face for a long time. "Honey, I think we need to leave town now. I really, really do."

"Two days, Mom."

"All right," she said. "I'll pick you up from that party on Saturday night. And if somebody else hasn't been arrested for killing Josh Emmit by then, we're getting on the Interstate and we're disappearing. Got it?"

"Got it."

We drove for a while, passing through Chinatown, past all these butcher shops with dead pigs and dead ducks and dead geese hanging in the windows. Finally Mom pulled up in front of my school and stopped the car. She started scrawling a note to the principal to explain why I was late for school. While she was writing, I thought about what I had just said. I had told her that I thought I knew who the killer was. I had just told her I had a plan for exposing the killer at The Hundred's party on Saturday night. But the truth was, I had next to nothing. Sometimes when you make up a story like that, though, it makes you think. Suddenly it occurred to me that maybe I *could* catch the killer in two days. Maybe I *could* trap them at the party. But how? It had something to do with this guy Mikhail Petrovich. I started getting excited.

"Have a nice day, sweetie," Mom said.

"Yeah." I hopped out of the car, started running toward the front door of school.

FOURTEEN

"WHERE'S ANNIE?" MARCO said.

Fabe had given me and Marco a ride to our gig in his *second* car—if you can believe that a nineteen-year-old kid owns two cars—one of these humongous Lincoln Navigators.

"She said she'd drive her own car," I said.

"Yeah, it's just . . ." Marco looked at his watch. "She said she'd be here fifteen minutes ago."

The rave or party or whatever you want to call it, was being held in the basement of this kind of hippie-dippy community center somewhere between Haight-Ashbury and the Mission District. There were all these artists' studios on the top floor, and then the basement was just this empty dark hole.

Fabe had an amazing amount of really nice equipment, including a hands-free wireless microphone setup that allowed me to sing without dragging a cord around. As he was hooking up the little transmitter to my microphone, clipping it to my pants, he looked over at Marco and said, "So you seem awful interested in Annie's whereabouts. Given how much you guys seem to hate each other."

"Huh?" Marco said.

Fabe looked at him for a minute. "Oh my God!" he said. "Shrimp, you're hot for Annie."

Marco blushed. "No, I'm not! And don't call me Shrimp."

"Oh, dude," he said. "It's all over your face."

"She's a total pain in the ass. How could I be hot for her?"

I chimed in. "Fabe's right. You talked about her every time I saw you at school today."

"You can all kiss my ass," Marco said.

We kept setting up. We were supposed to be starting at nine. By quarter to nine, I had started to worry. Annie still wasn't there.

Justin Bates, the guy who was organizing the thing, came up and said, "Dude, where's your bass player?"

"She'll be here," I said.

"You promised me a full band!" he said. "I can't pay you the full dose if you don't have a bass player."

"She'll *be* here," I said.

He gave me a look. I was thinking: *with all the crap I have to worry about, now this.*

"Welcome to being the leader of a band," Fabe said, grinning.

Justin Bates stood there glaring at me with his hands on his hips.

"Test, one, two," I said into my spiffy new wireless mic. "Check. Check."

Nine o'clock came and went. Still no Annie.

"Where the hell is she?" I said for about the fifth time. Now I was starting to get annoyed.

"It's cool," Fabe said. "Musicians are always late. I've been playing pro for five years, I bet I haven't been to five gigs that started on time."

I looked around the room. A fair number of kids had drifted into the room by now. Justin Bates had hooked a CD player up to our PA system, and music was booming out of the speakers—some band I'd never heard before.

"I'm gonna go outside and look," I said.

I went out in front of the arts center and looked around. Kids were wandering in. But I didn't see Annie anywhere. There was a mini-mall sort of thing around the corner, a park on the other side of the street. The kids who had driven were all parking their cars at the mini-mall. I walked around to the parking lot, still didn't see her. I was about to head back when I heard a horrible screeching noise. I whirled around and saw a bright purple Toyota pull into the other side of the parking lot, tires smoking. It looked like a typical dumb-ass boy car. Stickers with Japanese lettering on the windows, chrome wheels, purple neon around the license plate, a big wing on the back. It headed straight toward me, swerving at the last minute and slamming to a stop in a space just a few feet away from me.

The door opened, and it was Annie. She had blood coming out of her nose.

"My God," I said. "What happened?"

"Nothing," she said, stone-faced.

I could see bruises on her arms and the side of her neck. One eye was swollen almost shut. "Are you sure?"

"I said, it's *nothing*." She glared at me, pulling the case for her bass out of the trunk.

Annie's nose bled intermittently throughout the first whole set. After we had finished playing for the first hour,

I went and got a bag of ice, and Annie lay down on the floor on a wooden deck behind the building, the ice bag on her face. Music was blaring out the door. We didn't speak for about five minutes.

"You want to tell me about it?" I said finally.

Annie stared straight up at the ceiling. Finally she said, "It was a couple of Russian guys—a blond dude and a bald dude. They come up to me as I'm getting into my car and one of them is like, 'You a friend of Chass, huh?' I'm like, 'Who wants to know?' And he's like, BOOM!" She made a fist, punched the air. "The other guy grabs me, and they just beat on me for a while. After they were done, the big bald dude goes, 'Tell Chass if she keeps looking at this Josh Emmit thing, her mom's gonna be next. And it's gonna be a lot worse.'"

"Aw man," I said. I felt like throwing up. It was all my fault. Annie didn't have anything to do with this.

Annie sat up, took the ice bag away. "Don't you dare stop trying to find out what happened to Josh Emmit," she said. She shook the ice bag. There was a thin streak of blood running down the side of the bag. "This is nothing. I been through stuff a lot worse than this."

"I don't know what to say," I said again.

Annie's face was furious. "Don't say nothing," she said. She heaved the ice bag over the side of the wooden deck into a green Dumpster. "Let's go play some music."

As I was playing the second set, I noticed the guy from The Hundred come in. Neil Ostrov, Josh's friend. Now that he had his mask off, you could see clearly what a great-looking guy he was. He seemed to know a lot of kids—rapping knuckles, bumping shoulders, and hugging people left and right. It made me wonder how many of the kids in the room were members of The Hundred.

I've lived in a lot of towns. Columbus, Ohio. Prairie du Cheyne, Wisconsin. High Hopes, Alabama. Spokane, Washington. Just normal places. And the kids I've known all seemed pretty normal.

But San Francisco was different. The kids at this Real Music rave or party or whatever you want to call it— there was something different about them from the kids in Alabama or Wisconsin or whatever. It wasn't exactly that they were better dressed or better looking or richer— though those things were probably true. There was an expression in their eyes that was different. Like they'd seen more of the world. Like they were more confident, more certain, more sure of themselves. It was like the lights shone brighter on their faces than it did on the kids I was used to.

And I wasn't sure if that was a good thing or not.

About halfway into the set, Neil Ostrov wandered up to the front of the room and stood there watching me and smiling this mysterious smile. I don't think he took his eyes off me until the end of the set. Kids would come up to talk, and he would just wave them away. It's nice to get attention and all, but after a while, it kind of started creeping me out.

After we stopped playing, Neil walked up to me and said. "You look better without the Catwoman mask," he said.

"How did you know that was me?" I said.

He shrugged. "Little bird told me." He gestured with his hand to the group. "Great songs. Great voice. Great look. Great band. You're gonna be famous someday."

"You think?" I said lightly.

"No doubt." He was still smiling this mysterious smile at me. "So where are you from, Chass? I did a little asking around, nobody seems to know anything about you."

"I just moved here. From Alabama."

"Alabama. This must be a change."

"A little."

He laughed. "So. Josh gave you his number for Club Dread, huh?"

I didn't say anything.

"You been here a month or two. How'd you meet him?"

"A music thing," I said.

"Oh. A music thing." He smiled, but the smile wasn't in his eyes. "You're aware he's been on tour for the past two months?"

"Yeah, well, that's what happened," I said. "I met him while he was on the tour."

"He was touring in Japan. Not here. Not Alabama."

I looked at him for a minute and said, "Why all the questions?"

"Look, my job in The Hundred is to make sure all our members are legit. If Josh didn't really choose you, then you're not supposed to be there." He paused and his smile faded. "I happen to know for a fact that you weren't the one he chose. He had somebody else in mind."

"I wouldn't know anything about that," I said. "It seemed like he did it on the spur of the moment."

"Yeah. Uh-huh."

"While we're asking questions," I said, "where were you the night he was murdered?"

He stared at me. "What kind of question is that?"

"I'm just curious."

"Well it's a stupid question."

"The reason I'm curious," I said, "is because he owed you that sixty-three thousand dollars and—I don't know—I could imagine the cops might see that as some kind of motive for murder."

He blinked. It was obvious I'd taken him by surprise. Suddenly his smirky smile came back. "Oh! I see! You think, what, maybe you could frame me for murdering him or something? Win the game this year?"

"Not really," I said. "I don't care about that."

He laughed loudly, then moved closer to me. "If you think you can mess with me, shorty, think again."

"Sixty-three thousand bucks. That's a lot of money."

"For a guy like him? It's nothing."

"Yeah, but that's not the point, is it?" I said. "The question is, is it a lot of money for a guy like you?"

He didn't say anything.

"Speaking of which," I said. "Why *did* he owe you all that money?"

Neil glared at me. "I did not kill him. Josh was my best friend."

"Then what was all that pay-me-back-all-my-money-or-you're-going-to-get-your-legs-broken stuff?"

Neil's eyes narrowed.

"He left a tape," I said. "I mean, dude, basically you threatened his life."

Neil suddenly started looking nervous. "Bull."

"I'm serious. How about I show it to the cops, see what they think?"

Neil looked around the room, all fidgety now. "You got the tape?" he said.

"Yeah."

"How much do you want for it?"

"Tell me why he owed you all that money, Neil."

"It was a gambling thing. I take a few bets here and there. It's nothing."

"You mean you're like a, what do you call it? A bookie?"

"A thousand bucks. Give me the tape."

"I don't need a thousand bucks."

Neil's eyes bored holes in me. "You rich kids," he said angrily. "You think everybody just gets handed money. Well, it doesn't work that way, sweetie. Some of us have to earn it."

"You ever thought about working at Wal-Mart instead of being an illegal bookie?"

He snorted.

"I don't know," I said. "It still sounds like you did it."

"I have an alibi."

"Tell me where you were," I said. "If you have a legit alibi, I'll look for somebody else to, uh . . . to frame."

He narrowed his eyes. "My parents own a restaurant. I wait tables at the restaurant. I was there the whole night. My name is on all the receipts."

"What's the restaurant called?"

"Give it up, Chass. You're wasting your time. You're not gonna win the game this way."

"What's the restaurant called?"

"You want to frame somebody, you ought to try that no-talent loser Will Gaffney. *There's* a guy with motive. He pretended he was Josh's little buddy, doing everything Josh said. But the truth is, he hated Josh. He was working twenty-four-seven trying to screw Josh, trying to get the record company to drop Josh so they'd concentrate on making *him* into a star."

"The restaurant," I said. "What's the restaurant called?"

"You're not listening to me."

"The. Restaurant."

"I give up," Neil said. "It's called the Ukranian Peasant."

He turned and walked away from me. The Ukranian Peasant.

I turned around, saw Annie looking at me curiously.

"The guys who beat you up," I said. "How did you know they were Russian?"

"The way they talked."

"What about Ukranian?" I said. "Could they have been Ukranian?"

"Ukranian, Russian—what's the difference?" She put her hand gently up to her nose. When she pulled it away, there was a drop of blood on one of her fingers. "Aw crap, it's bleeding again."

FIFTEEN

AS WE WERE about to start the next set, I spotted a man walking into the back of the room who looked completely out of place. He wore a long black leather trench coat and was about twenty years older than anybody else at the party. He walked up to the stage where I was standing. It was Will's manager, Mikhail Petrovich.

"So, Chass," he said, "you get my message?"

"What message?" I said.

He pointed at Annie's face, then smirked at me.

I turned and saw Annie speaking quietly to Marco.

Marco's face suddenly got hard and he came around, stood in front of Will's manager.

"Did you do this?" Marco said to Mikhail Petrovich.

The huge Ukranian looked down at Marco and laughed. "What. You gonna do something about it, little boy?"

Marco didn't say anything, but suddenly his leg lashed out, catching the big Ukranian right between the legs. It wasn't like a soft little kick either. He just whaled the crap out of the guy. Mikhail Petrovich grunted and his eyes went wide. Then he fell over on the floor, moaning and holding his crotch.

Marco looked down at the moaning Ukranian and said, "See this girl? Her name is Annie. She's my friend. You mess with my friends, you're messing with me."

At about that moment Will appeared.

"What happened to Mikhail?" he said.

"He had an accident," I said.

Will grabbed his manager, helped him to his feet. "This isn't over," Mikhail grunted, pointing a shaking finger at Marco. "You gonna be sorry, little boy."

"Something tells me that wasn't very smart," Fabe said.

Annie put her arm around Marco. "Yeah it was really dumb," she said. Then she kissed him on the side of his face. "But it was *so* cool."

152

Marco got a kind of funny expression on his face, then looked around the room. "Isn't our break about over?" he said.

About two songs into the third set, we pretty much ran out of material. We'd only had a few days to rehearse, so we just didn't have four sets' worth of songs. I got all nervous about it and kept apologizing to the audience until Fabe told me, "Don't apologize. Nobody's really paying attention. And even if they are, they don't care."

It was good advice. I looked out at the crowd of kids. There were maybe a couple of people who were actually paying attention to the music—mostly lonely-looking boys—but pretty much everybody else was dancing or talking. For the fourth set, we played the whole first set over. Same songs, same order—and not one person complained.

Except Justin Bates, the promoter of the event, who came up after we were done and said, "So, look, the crowd was a little light today. I hate to do this, but I can't pay you quite as much as I promised."

"What do you mean?" I said.

Fabe came up and stood over Justin. "Yeah, what do you mean?"

"Look, I'm trying to be fair and everything," Justin said, "but . . ."

"But basically," Fabe said, "you're trying to screw us."

"Dude, you played a bunch of the same songs twice!" Justin was suddenly sounding like the whole thing was our fault. "Your bass player showed up late. Your drummer started a fight."

"Yeah," I said, "but we played four sets, four hours, just like we promised."

"Look, I'd be within my rights, docking you for the fighting and everything. I'm trying to be fair here but—"

"But you're trying to rip us off," Marco said.

Justin sighed. "Dude, I'd love to use you guys again. But this isn't like a regular nightclub or whatever. You can't get blood from a stone."

"How much are you talking?" I said.

He took out a bunch of bills and set them on top of my music stand. I couldn't really even guess how much it was.

"Oh, come *on*!" Fabe said.

"Guys, guys," Justin said. "I'm doing my best!"

"You need to do better," Annie said.

Justin started patting his pockets, pulling out wadded-up bills and adding them to the stack he'd already given us. "That's all I got," he said. Then he walked away.

Marco scooped up the bills, straightened them, counted them, split them into four piles.

"Forty-seven bucks apiece," he said with a sour smile.

My heart sank. "Oh, man, I'm such a crappy band leader," I said. "I'm sorry. I'm so sorry. He promised me six hundred on the phone and then . . ."

Fabe put his arm around me. "Welcome to the music business," he said. "Get used to it."

After we'd packed up our instruments and equipment, Annie said, "Hey, check this out."

"What?" I said.

She smiled mysteriously and started walking across the parking lot, pausing in front of a white BMW. She reached into her purse, pulled out her car keys, and started walking slowly down the side of the car. She dragged the key along the side of the car, ripping a jagged line of paint off the side of the car.

"What are you doing?" I said.

"That's Justin Bates's car," she said.

Even though I felt a little bad about it, I couldn't help myself: I started laughing and laughing.

I laughed all the way back to the other side of the parking lot where Annie's and Fabe's cars were parked. Just then a big car pulled off the main street nearby and started driving toward us. Immediately I stopped laughing, and my heart started racing.

"Let's get in the car," I said.

"What's wrong?" Marco said.

"Just get in the car," I said.

Marco shrugged, got into Annie's car. Fabe got into his SUV and started the motor. I climbed into Annie's car, Annie started the motor. I could see the big car on the other side of the parking lot creeping toward us.

"Let's *go*," I said.

"All right already," Annie said.

It wasn't until we had hit the street that I realized what it was about the big car on the other side of the lot that scared me. It was a red car. Something about it made me think it was the same car that was driven by whoever had shot Josh Emmit.

I turned, looked behind us. The red car had turned out of the parking lot and was half a block behind us.

"Turn at the light," I said.

"Yeah but that's not the way to—"

"Just do what I said," I snapped.

Annie shrugged. At the light she paused, turned just as the light was about to turn red. I kept watching behind us. The big car blew right through the red light, picked up speed as it headed toward us.

"Somebody's following us," I said.

"Not for long," Annie said. The way she said it, it was like she thought this was fun. Then she leaned across me, picked up a pair of black driving gloves off the dashboard, the kind with the fingers cut out, pulled them on her hands.

"You think it's that Russian dude I kicked in the nuts?" Marco said.

"I don't know." I paused. "Whoever it is, though, I think it's the same person that shot Josh Emmit."

"You're kidding," Marco said, his voice cracking a little.

Annie, however, seemed unperturbed. In fact, she let her speed drop until the red car was almost on us. I couldn't see anybody's face through the windshield of the red car, just the reflection of streetlights on glass.

"What are you *doing*?" I said. "Go! Go!"

"I want to make it fair," she said.

"Fair?" I shouted.

The red car had almost reached us. It swerved sharply out into the oncoming lane, pulled around us, then swerved again and slammed on its brakes, cutting us off.

Annie smiled. "Nice try, bitch," she said.

She braked too, then suddenly dropped the car into reverse, then floored it. I don't know what kind of motor she had in that thing, but it wasn't the normal motor they put in at the factory. The car peeled out backward, tires shrieking and skidding, throwing up a huge cloud of white smoke. Then my head snapped sideways as Annie cut the wheel sharply, and we spun around in a half circle.

By the time the car had stopped spinning, she had the car in first gear. This time when she dropped the clutch, she didn't smoke the tires. Instead the car just threw us back in the seats. The acceleration was so hard, it felt like somebody had their hand on my face, shoving me back into the seat.

I looked behind me. As we reached the traffic light, the red car burst out of the cloud of smoke Annie's tires had left and was barreling toward us. I turned around, looked at the speedometer. We were already going sixty-five on this dinky little city street, and Annie still had the accelerator smashed all the way to the floor.

"Three hundred and twelve horses of pure turbo-charged intercooled JDM power!" Annie yelled.

"What's that mean?" I said.

"It means she's out of her mind," Marco said.

The speedometer hit ninety at the next light, a hundred and five at the third. The red car was about half a block behind us now, keeping pace.

"He's got nothing," Annie said. The next light was turning red in front of us.

"Annie, Annie, Annie!" I said. I don't know if I was more terrified of Annie's driving or of whoever was in the car behind us.

Annie didn't say anything, but when we were about a hundred yards from the light, she suddenly slammed on the brakes, cut the wheel slightly. By the time we were approaching the light, the whole car was traveling sideways at about fifty miles an hour, the tires howling like a dying dog. I was pretty sure we were going to die. Annie, however, didn't look at all worried. In fact, she was grinning, her black eyes glittering in the streetlights.

Cars were slamming on brakes and honking. About the time we reached the middle of the cross street, the wheels suddenly got purchase on the road and, boom, we were traveling in another direction on another street. Unfortunately we were in the oncoming lane with car headlights aimed straight at us. The car in front of us peeled off just as we were about to hit it. Annie calmly nudged the steering wheel and got us back in the correct lane.

"Oh-ho-hooooo," Marco said. "That was awesome!"

"What are you," I said, "some kind of race car driver?"

"Something like that," she said.

"Oh my god," Marco said. "You're a drifter, aren't you?"

"What's a drifter?" I said.

"It's a motor sport," Annie said primly.

"It's like a bunch of crazy idiots who drive cars around a parking lot and see who can skid the most," Marco said.

"No, in fact, drifting is a totally legitimate motor sport," Annie said primly.

I looked behind us. The big red car had dropped back half a block. Annie stomped on the gas, but the big red car started gaining on us. Meanwhile we were tearing through intersections at close to a hundred miles an hour on roads where nobody in their right mind would drive more than about forty.

"He's got a big engine in there," Annie said. "We're gonna have to beat him on agility."

"What's that mean?" I said.

"More going around corners sideways at sixty miles an hour," Marco said.

"I think I'm just going to close my eyes," I said.

But I couldn't.

"You ever see that movie *Bullitt*?" Annie said.

"No," I said.

"Steve McQueen. The greatest car chase of all time. Let's check out Taylor Street, see how his suspension holds up."

"What is she talking about, Marco?" I said.

Marco looked a little pale. "You'll see," he said.

We screeched around a corner, and suddenly we were way up on this steep road heading down toward the bay. At each intersection, there was a huge bump. Behind us I could see the big red car, leaning heavily as it came around the corner. Annie accelerated. I felt my stomach stay up at the top of the hill. We took the first bump, and Annie's car went airborne. It seemed like we were flying for hours. I was beyond terrified now.

The car smashed down on the ground, metal jangling and crashing.

"Hmm," Annie said.

I got the feeling that "hmm" meant something not good.

Behind us the red car went airborne too. It landed with a huge crash, fishtailing a little and sending a shower of sparks into the road behind it.

And then we were airborne again. My stomach came up into my throat.

SMASH!

The red car had dropped back a little. It went airborne again, but not quite as high this time. Again it smashed down hard. This time an exhaust pipe spun out into the road behind it.

The was another bump, and we were flying again.

SMASH!

"Hmm," Annie said again.

"I don't like it when she says that," Marco said.

"Neither do I," I said.

Then we were flying.

SMASH!

This time is was Annie's exhaust pipe that was spinning and clattering down the road. It banged off the red car's grille, leaving a big dent. Marco whooped.

Airborne again. I was starting to feel sick.

SMASH!

The red car was over a block and a half behind us, creeping over the bumps now.

"That's right, bitch," Annie said. "Now you know how the big girls play."

We went airborne.

This time when we came down, the SMASH! was accompanied by a worrisome clatter, and the car seemed to stagger and lean to the left.

"Hmmmm," Annie said. "Maybe that's about enough of that."

She stomped on the brakes and turned at the next light, doing her usual routine, skidding around the corner about ten times faster than they tell you to do it in driver's ed class.

As we came around the corner, I saw the police car. And apparently it saw us too, because it turned on its flashers, hung a U-turn, and started following us.

"What do you think?" Annie said. "Should I outrun the cops too?"

"Oh God," I said.

But she put on her blinker and pulled over.

Behind us I saw the red car turn and slow. It crept up to us, then passed us as the policeman climbed out of his car. I tried to make out a face, but the windows were slightly tinted, and I couldn't see anything at all. I could feel someone watching me, though. As soon as it had gotten all the way around us, the red car picked up speed and zoomed off into the night, something under the car dragging on the ground leaving a trail of sparks.

"Chrysler Three Hundred, California licence GLX 435," Annie whispered.

"Huh?" I said.

"The red car. The license number is GLX 435."

Behind us, the policeman had his hand on his holster as he approached the car.

"You know, Chass," Annie whispered, "every police cruiser has a computer hookup to the DMV. If somebody could get in there, they run the tag number and find out who owns that car."

"Yeah, but how would we do that?" I said.

The policeman leaned over, shining his flashlight on each of us in turn. He was a really huge guy, with hairy wrists and giant weight-lifter arms.

Annie cocked her head and smiled flirtatiously at the policeman. "Something wrong, officer?" she said.

"Let me see your license and proof of insurance."

"Well, gosh, you know what?" Annie said. "Unfortunately, I'm an underage driver, I have no license, and this crappy old heap is totally uninsured."

The cop's eyes narrowed. He looked at her for about ten seconds, his hand still resting on his gun butt. "You want to step out of the car, young lady?" he said.

"I'd be happy to," she said. Then she leaned over, took a pen out of her pocket, and wrote something on my wrist.

"Now!" the policeman said.

She leaned down, took off her heels, then climbed out of the car. I looked down at my wrist. GLX 435.

"I'm not sure I like the looks of this," Marco said.

"Step over here, place your hands on the side of the car," the policeman said to Annie.

"You know what she's about to do, don't you?" Marco said.

I shook my head.

"I guess I better help." Marco sighed loudly, then opened his door.

"Get back in the car, son," the cop said.

As he focused his attention on Marco, Annie bolted, heading off down the street.

"Hey!" Marco yelled. "Dude! Check this out." He turned, yanked his pants down, mooning the cop. Then he started running in the opposite direction, laughing like a maniac.

The big policeman looked at him, then at Annie, hesitated for a moment, then took off after Marco.

Okay, I was thinking. This is not good.

But then I climbed out of the car and stood for a minute. Marco had disappeared around one corner, Annie around the other. The night was quiet. The police car's blue lights threw weird shadows up and down the street. But other than the lights, nothing moved.

I looked down at my wrist. GLX 435. There it was.

I took a deep breath, walked over to the police car, climbed in. Just like Annie had said, there was a computer terminal sprouting out of the dashboard of the cruiser. I looked at the menu. There were a bunch of menu options. The third one down said: DMV.

I clicked on it. The next menu had a place for make, model, one that said DL#, something that said VIN, and something else that said CA TAG. I typed GLX 435 into the little box that said CA TAG, hit the return key.

It seemed like it took forever for the computer to bring back a name. I just sat there, staring and staring. Suddenly the screen went blank, and then a name popped up.

"What!" I said.

Before I had a chance to make sense of what I was seeing, the door flew open. The big cop had his gun out, pointing it right at my chest. "Out of the car!" he screamed. "On the ground! Out of the car! On the ground, now!"

"Okay, *okay!*" I said.

SIXTEEN

IT WAS TWO-THIRTY in the morning when my mom finally arrived at the police station.

"You want to tell me what's going on?" she said. "I had to leave work in the middle of the shift, and that greasy little Andre creep is probably going to fire me."

I could tell Mom was pissed. And I couldn't blame her. "You're not gonna believe," I said.

"I'm not going to believe what?"

"I found out who killed Josh Emmit."

"That's nice, sweetie," she said. "But guess what?"

"What?"

"I turned on the ten o'clock news, and guess whose face was right there in the middle of a story about Josh Emmit?"

"I don't know."

"Yours," Mom said.

I blinked. "But . . ."

"They didn't give your name, they just said, 'This juvenile has been questioned repeatedly regarding the case.' And there was your face."

"I don't know what to say," I said.

"Well, it doesn't matter. I don't think they're going to require bail for whatever you did tonight. They're going to let me take you away, and then you and I are getting in the car and we're leaving."

"Mom!" I said. "Did you even listen to what I said? I just told you I know who killed Josh Emmit."

"Sure, that's great. And I'm sure the nice cop who gave you his word that he wouldn't talk to the press about you and then proceeded to immediately leak your picture to them—I suppose he's going to take your information down and then go out and arrest the perpetrator. Right?"

"Did they use my name?" I said.

Mom didn't answer.

"So they put my face on TV on some local news

show. Big deal. How's Kyle Van Epps going to find out about that? It's not like he lives in San Francisco."

"If a local station has your picture today, it'll be on CNN tomorrow."

"Mom!"

"No. This is settled. We're leaving town the minute I get you out of here."

"Well," I said, "I don't know what to tell you."

"It's not a matter of telling me or not telling me. The decision is made."

I don't fight with my mom all that much. Sure, we get into it now and then. But compared to most kids, I get along pretty well with my mother. But as I was sitting there I was feeling like I just couldn't bear to do what she wanted—to disappear, change my name, change my school, change my address, for the umpteenth time. It was just too much. Especially because I felt like I now knew who had actually killed Josh Emmit. If I *knew*, then it was just a matter of time. Right?

So I just slumped down in my chair and sat there, staring at the wall.

After a while the big policeman who had arrested me came in the room wearing his wraparound sunglasses and said that I was being let off with a warning. He gave me this big speech about if I kept hanging out with bad kids and getting in trouble I'd end up in prison and all this crap, and then he took off his sunglasses and started sweet-talking Mom, trying to get her phone number and staring at her chest.

As we walked out of the station house, Mom said, "Are you planning on saying thank you?"

"I should thank your boobs," I said. "That's why that policeman let me go."

"Yeah, but I'm the one who carried them here at two-thirty in the morning," she said.

As we were walking out, I saw a car I recognized sitting at the curb. It was Annie's souped-up little Toyota. And Annie was sitting in the front seat. She spotted me and waved.

"You need a ride?" she yelled.

Mom looked at me for a minute and then said, "You can go tell her good-bye," she said. "Then we're going straight home and we're getting out of here."

I walked over to Annie's car, and my heart was hammering in my chest. I just felt like I couldn't do it. I didn't really care much about San Francisco or my apartment or my school. But this band was *mine*. It was mine like nothing I'd ever had before.

"Hey," I said. "How come you're here?"

"I got away from the cops, but they caught Marco

170

too," she said. "I'm here to pick him up. He called his parents and said he was spending the night with Fabe, so they don't even know he got popped."

"Oh, okay."

"Is that your mom?" Annie said.

"Yeah."

"So I guess you don't need a ride, huh?"

I didn't answer.

I stood there for a minute, not saying anything. Then I looked back at Mom. She was standing there, looking all grim and businesslike—the way she always does before we split town—and I suddenly just thought: *no*. Every time she's said we had to go, I've left my life, my name, my personal photographs, my friends, and all that other stuff behind. But this time? Nope. Wasn't gonna do it.

I walked around and climbed in the front seat of Annie's car.

Annie leaned down, looking curiously at me.

"Go," I said.

"Huh? But—what about your mom? And how am I going to explain this to Marco?"

"Just *go*," I said.

"What am I, your limo driver for the night."

"Go!"

She shrugged, started the car, drove off rapidly down the road. I didn't look back. But I could imagine Mom back there, watching me go. She was bound to be totally flipping out. I had never done anything like this in my life. I've always been a good kid, always seeing things from Mom's perspective, always doing what I was told.

But not today.

We drove for a while, and finally I said, "So, you think I could spend the night with you?"

"Hmm . . . ," she said.

"That's what you said when your car was about to smash to bits on that hill," I said.

She didn't say anything.

"Never mind," I said. "I know, it's probably a problem for your parents or something."

Still she didn't say anything. My cell phone rang. I looked at the number. It was Mom. I didn't answer. It kept ringing, so after a while I turned it off. We kept driving for a while. I didn't really know San Francisco all that well, but I had the impression we weren't driving anywhere in particular but were just kind of driving around randomly.

Finally we ended up in this industrial-looking area. Annie pulled up under a bridge and stopped. She didn't say anything, just sat there staring out the windshield. There was this funny glint in her eyes, like she was about to cry. Only the tears weren't coming out.

"What?" I said finally.

She shook her head.

"Is it about getting beat up today?" I said. "I'm sorry about that. I feel like such a jerk. I'm sucking everybody into my problems."

"I don't care about that," she said, her voice flat and kind of tired-sounding.

"Then what is it?"

"Remember when I said I wasn't homeless?"

I nodded.

"You probably figured, I've got nice clothes, a cool car, I must have a nice family and everything."

I shrugged.

She motioned around us at the dark concrete. I could hear the traffic lumbering over us, thudding against the concrete.

"I was lying," she said. She sounded as sad as anybody I've ever heard. "This is it. Home sweet home."

I looked at the dirty shell of concrete around us, and I couldn't figure out for a minute what she meant. "Annie . . . What . . ."

"I spent like the first five or six years of my life in this refugee camp in Thailand," she said. "My dad died when I was little. Me and Mom moved over here. Then Mom got sick too. Something went wrong at the hospital, and she died. I was fourteen at the time. I tried to make money picking up cans and all that stuff, but after a while

I couldn't make enough money to pay the rent. I got evicted. I didn't want to end up in the system, get stuck in some crap foster home or whatever. So all I had was Mom's car. I started living in it about two years ago."

"Annie."

"It's okay." She smiled. But it was a sad smile. "I love my car." She laughed bitterly. "I still pick up cans to make money. And you know what I do with the money? Instead of getting a place to live? I buy new parts for my car. Isn't that queer? I guess there's something wrong with me."

"God, Annie, you're only like sixteen years old. You're not supposed to be worrying about buying groceries and paying rent and stuff."

"You should go back to your mom," she said. She sounded a little angry now. "Maybe she's mad. But at least she's there."

"It's not that," I said. "It's complicated."

"Whatever." Annie kept staring out the window. After a while the tears started running down her face. But she didn't make any noise, and her face hardly had any expression on it at all. "Just don't tell Marco," she said.

"I won't."

"'Cause I think I'm kind of digging him, you know? I thought he was a little asshole at first. But then? When he kicked that Russian dude in the nuts? It was like he was defending me. I never had anybody do anything like that for me before."

"Ukranian," I said.

"If he thought I was just some little weird homeless chick that picks up cans to buy food, he'd be like, *pshhhh*." She waved her hand dismissively. After a minute she leaned her car seat back. "There're some blankets in the backseat."

The car was starting to get a little cold. It seemed like it was never warm in San Francisco. I pulled a blanket out of the backseat and wrapped it around me, leaned the seat back. I kept thinking about Mom, about how lonely and scared she must be. Just like me. I started to get my cell phone out and call her. But I couldn't do it.

After a while I could tell by the way she was breathing that Annie was sleeping. I tried to sleep, too, but it never came.

SEVENTEEN

"TROY HOLLIWELL," I said.

"Who?" Annie said, rubbing her eyes sleepily. We were still sitting under the grimy concrete overpass, the early morning light slanting into our faces.

"The car that chased us has to be the guy that killed Josh Emmit. And the guy who owns the car is named Troy Holliwell."

"Well, who is he?"

"Yeah," I said. "That's the thing. I have no idea."

"So what are you going to do?"

"Well, I've got a couple ideas," I said. "But first I better go home."

Annie dropped me off at my apartment, and I walked up to the door with my heart in my throat. I was sure Mom was going to kill me.

I put the key in the lock, walked in. "Mom?" I called.

No answer. The apartment was dark, the curtains drawn. My eyes strained to adjust to the darkness. I flipped on the light switch, but it was broken.

"Mom. I'm home."

As I turned around to lock the door, I heard something behind me. I couldn't quite make out what it was—just a stirring of cloth on cloth, like a person shifting slightly in a chair.

I whirled around. For the first time I noticed something different about the living room. A shape in the dark that wasn't supposed to be there.

"Don't worry," a voice said. "I won't hurt you."

The light came on then—a lamp on the other side of the room—and the dark shape turned into a man. He wasn't especially scary looking. He was kind of skinny, and wore baggy cargo pants and a T-shirt imprinted with the name of some video game that I'd never heard of. I figured he was in his early twenties—but it was hard to tell because his hair was snow-white. He had strange blue eyes that were so pale they almost seemed white. Suddenly I felt like I couldn't breathe.

"Where's my mom?" I said.

"That's what I was wondering," the pale young man said. He had a high, grating voice.

"Who are you?"

He smiled in what I'm sure was supposed to be a pleasant and reassuring way. Only it came off creepy. "I'm sorry, Chass, I should introduce myself." He rose from the chair. "My name is Troy Holliwell."

He took a step toward me.

"I'll scream," I said. "I swear. Don't touch me."

"Hey, hey, whoa!" He held his hands up like somebody was pointing a gun at his head. "I know I kind of surprised you. But I'm just here to interview your mom."

I frowned at him, puzzled. "To *what*?"

"In-ter-view." He said in a slow, snide cadence. "Do I need to define the word for you?"

I just looked at him.

"Troy *Holliwell*?" he said. "*The* Troy Holliwell? In all modesty I'm like, kind of famous. You've never heard of me?"

"Nope."

"Troy Holliwell? The crusading journalist?" He waited vainly for a glimmer of recognition. "I'm with *The Rag*, America's number one alternative newspaper."

"'Fraid I missed that one," I said.

He shook his head like I was a total idiot. "Yeah, well, whatever. Anyway, point is, I'm an investigative reporter based in Los Angeles. I've been trying to find your mom for like years now. And she keeps dodging me." He waved me over to the couch. "Come on. Sit down. I won't bite."

I was torn. On the one hand, I didn't trust this guy. So far as I knew, he had shot Josh Emmit. But at the same time, he didn't seem all that threatening. He seemed more like an annoying computer nerd than anything else. And besides, I might be able to get some information—maybe even a confession out of him if I stayed in the room.

I sat on the couch, as far from him as possible, put my hand inside my purse. "Just so you know," I said. "I have a knife." I didn't. But I figured it couldn't hurt saying I did.

"Yeah, whatever."

"So why are you looking for my mom?" I said.

"You ever hear of a guy named Kyle Van Epps?"

Kyle Van Epps was the reason Mom and I had been running all my life. But I decided to be cagey. "Isn't he the president of some company?" I said.

"That would be Apex Global Media," he said. "The largest media empire in the world."

"Oh," I said. "Yeah."

"I've been working on a book about Apex and Kyle Van Epps for several years now. The guy's a total scumbag. He's been using his control of his magazines and TV stations and newspapers and so on to influence politicians and do all kinds of scummy stuff. But I've always had a hunch there was more going on. It was like I kept banging up against this wall of fear and intimidation that he used to keep people in line. But I found a bunch of leads that kept heading toward this mysterious woman. I couldn't figure out her name, but every time I'd get close, it was obvious it was the same woman. One time she worked in accounting for a division of Apex. Another time she worked in another part of the company. Another time she was arrested for trespassing. And every time, there'd be a different name, a different story as to who she was. And every time she appeared, she'd be gone without a trace."

I shrugged noncommitally.

"There were two things I'd always find out about this mystery woman," Troy Holliwell continued. "One, she was a total babe. Everybody always said that. Wherever she'd been, I could always find three or four guys with their tongues still hanging out. And the other thing I found out was that she had a daughter." He smiled at me. "You seem to have made a big impression in the last town where you guys lived. Little town in Alabama. I mean I admit that the bumpkins down there are probably easily impressed and all. But everybody said, 'Wow, that Chass, she was one fabulous singer. She's gonna be famous someday.'"

"So how did you find us?"

"That's what I'm telling you. My paper, *The Rag*, is part of a chain of alternative papers that are published in a whole bunch of cities. Most of them have very extensive entertainment listings. Nightclubs, coffeehouses, the acts that are playing, all that stuff. And all the listings are databased on our main computer. I just went to the IT department, asked them to run a search for the word *Chass* in the nightclub listings. I found three coffeehouses in San Francisco that had booked a singer named Chass. So I got in my car, drove up here from LA, started going around to the coffeehouses where you were booked to play. One of them points at this blue poster and goes, 'Oh, yeah, Chass was just in here about half an hour ago putting up posters.' So I drove around until I spotted this cute blond girl putting up a blue poster on the window of a coffeehouse."

I was looking at his face really carefully, trying to see if it seemed like he was lying. I couldn't really tell. But the story seemed reasonable so far.

"Anyway, I'm looking for a parking space—which

there don't seem to be any of in this whole stupid city—
when I hear this *bang bang*. I look in the mirror, and I
see this dude fall down and there's blood on the window
and stuff and I'm like, *Holy moly, I better get back there
and see what's going on.* So I start backing up, and when
I get about ten feet away from you, you start hauling ass
down the street.

"Then I look over and I'm like, *Oh my God!* Because
I recognize the dude slumped over on the ground is like
Josh Emmit. Right? And I'm thinking, whoa, what's going on? By that time you had disappeared around the corner. So I'm figuring, *You know what?—I don't need to be
hanging around here getting questioned by the cops.* I
don't know what it is about me, but cops hate me."

"Your really annoying attitude, maybe?" I said.

He glared at me then went on: "Anyway, by that
time, you've disappeared around the corner. I didn't
feel like backing up on a one-way street and having the
cops get all over my ass—who am I, what am I doing
here, did I witness the crime, pulling my criminal record,
so on and so forth—so I head out, drive around the
neighborhood looking for you. But by that time, you
were gone."

I sat there for a while, chewing over what he'd just
told me. If he was telling the truth—and his story
sounded reasonable enough—then the whole red car

thing had been a total dead-end waste of time. I was back to square one.

"That *was* you chasing us last night, right?"

"Sure," he said.

"Why?"

"Dude, this the biggest story I've ever worked on. I was just trying to find your mom."

"But—"

"After you got pulled over, I checked the police station. Turned out you'd been arrested! Paid the cop who arrested you twenty bucks, he gave me your address. And now here I am.

"So," he said briskly, "where's your mom?"

"Uh . . . ," I said. What I knew was that if Mom knew that somebody was looking to plaster her story across the front page of some newspaper, we'd definitely be in our car and heading down the road in about thirteen seconds. "She's, um, out of town for the weekend," I said.

"Where is she?"

"You wasted a trip," I said. "She's in LA right now."

"Doing what?"

"How should I know?"

He drummed his fingers on the coffee table for a minute. "Where's she staying?"

"I don't know."

"Got a phone number?"

I just looked at him.

"What?"

"How dumb do you think I am, Troy?"

"Look, we can help each other!" he said urgently. "It's obvious your mom has something on Kyle Van Epps. Otherwise why would you guys have spent all these years moving around and changing your names."

I didn't speak.

"I'm right, aren't I?"

Again, I just sat there.

"What is it? What did Kyle Van Epps do? What is it that's kept you guys on the run all these years?"

I sat there for a long time, thinking. The problem was this: if he showed up asking Mom to talk, it was a sure bet that Mom would flee. And my band would be down the toilet. I had to get rid of this guy. Permanently.

Finally I said, "How much do you know about mental illness?"

He looked at me through narrowed eyes. "Are you implying I'm crazy?"

I tried to look really sincere. "This isn't about you, Troy. I'm being serious."

"What do I need to know about mental illness."

"You ever read about bipolar disorder?"

"Manic depression. One day you're all hyped up and excited, the next day you want to kill yourself."

"Kinda," I said. When I was about thirteen, I had gone through a phase where I'd thought maybe my mom was nuts, that we had been running all these years for nothing. So I had gone to the library in the town where we lived at the time, read every book they had about mental illness. It turned out Mom was perfectly sane, but I remembered a lot of details about the stuff I'd read. "See, Troy, the way this bipolar thing affects some people, when they go through their manic phase, it's not like they just get real happy or something. There's all kind of weird stuff that happens. Grandiose delusions. That's where you think you're a lot more important than you are. Paranoia. That's where you think people are out to get you. Hallucinations. All kinds of weird stuff."

"What's this got to do with your mom?"

"My mom suffers from bipolar disorder with obsessive-compulsive tendencies. Big time. When she's on her medicine—which is about half the time—she's totally normal. But when she's off? Then she's really depressed and suicidal for a month or so out of the year. And the rest of the time she's has this ongoing delusion that she is being persecuted by Kyle Van Epps."

"So wait a minute. You really do know who Kyle Van Epps is."

"After spending my entire life with somebody who's obsessed with the guy? Dude, I can tell you what his favorite cologne is and what he eats for breakfast. That doesn't mean I know anything that's gonna help your story."

"Chass." He gave me this irritating smile and started talking to me like I was four years old. "My research indicates your mom has been investigating Kyle Van Epps for over five years."

"Your research is way off. She's been doing it for sixteen years."

"Chass. Look. Five years, sixteen years, whatever. You're talking about focus, discipline, long-term commitment. A crazy person just couldn't pull that off."

"Of course they could. That's precisely what a crazy person would do." I pulled out a detail from my memory banks. "Go look it up in the *DSM* Five."

"The what?"

"The *DSM* Five. Diagnostic Something-or-other Manual, Fifth Edition. I forget what it stands for exactly. It's basically like this manual that psychiatrists use. Here comes somebody that's all whacked out in this way or that way, you flip through it till you find all the symptoms, and, bam, there's the name for that condition." I pointed at my computer over in the corner of the room. "You can pull it up on the Internet. Look under bipolar with OCD."

"OCD?"

"Have you been listening, Troy? OCD. Obsessive-compulsive disorder. It's all right there in black and white. The good news about bipolar-with-OCD people? Funny, enthusiastic, charming, exciting, frequently very attractive to the opposite sex. The bad news? Long-standing grandiose delusions, paranoia, goofy obsessions that last years and years and years, secretiveness, blah blah blah. I'm sixteen years old. Could I make this stuff up? It's all right there in the book. Practically has my mom's picture printed in the margin."

I could see the reporter deflating like a balloon. His voice went quiet. "You're serious."

"Dude, I've spent my whole life taking care of a crazy person. You want to sit here for a while, I could spend the whole freaking morning telling you how much my life sucks."

He looked desperate now. "There's something. You know there is. She's got to have *something* on Kyle Van Epps. She didn't settle on him out of the blue."

"Look, Troy, here's what I *can* tell you. My mom's real name is Jenna Farmer." I figured the best lie always has a pinch of truth. "She was a singer. She did her first album on Argonaut Records right before I was born. Back then Kyle Van Epps was head of the record label. This was before he became head of Apex. Anyway, Mom started acting all weird, and Kyle Van Epps dropped her from the label. I guess that's when she had her first psychotic break. And when he dropped her from the label, she fixated on him."

"I don't believe this. I do not believe this." He was running his fingers through his white hair, making it stand up like Einstein's.

"Look it up, *Rolling Stone, Spin,* all the music magazines, sixteen years ago. Singer-songwriter Jenna Farmer. Promising career, first album gets good reviews, yadda yadda. Then . . ." I snapped my fingers. "She falls off the map."

"Yeah but—"

"You want to know the stories I've heard? Okay, Kyle Van Epps is an embezzler, he's a pedophile, he's a heroin smuggler, he's an agent for Osama bin Laden, he's keeping children imprisoned under his house and serving them up as sausage to guests at his fancy parties . . ." I slapped my hands flat on the table. "You want me to go on? It all depends on how sick she is."

The reporter slumped back in his chair.

"Look," I said, "truth is, Mom's not out of town. She's a waitress, and she's been working the night shift at Denny's. She should be home any minute. If you stay here, she will latch onto you and incorporate you into all her paranoid fantasies, and you will spend the next twenty years changing your phone number so that she'll stop hounding you with all the crazy stuff she's making up about Kyle Van Epps."

"Oh man! Oh, this so totally sucks! I've spent three *years* tracking her down!"

"Bummer."

"This can't be happening!" He kept running his hands through his hair.

"You better go." I said. "She'll be home in like five minutes. If she gets here you are *so* screwed."

He stood up hurriedly, went to the door, and then suddenly stopped like he'd thought of something. My heart sank. I wanted to be rid of him in the biggest kind of way.

"Hey," he said, "meant to ask you. This Josh Emmit thing."

"Yeah . . ."

"Did the cops ever talk to you?"

"Uh . . . Yeah."

He looked puzzled. "'Cause I was kind of surprised they hadn't arrested anybody."

"Why?"

"Well. I mean the shooter was sitting right there."

I blinked.

"What," he said. "You didn't see them?"

I shook my head.

"Yeah, Chass. They were sitting right there in a car across the street. I would have thought you'd have seen it."

"No. My back was turned when the shots were fired."

"Yeah, she pulled out in front of me after she fired the shots. Nearly ran into me."

"*She?*"

"You sure I didn't mention this earlier? I thought I had. Yeah, she had a gun in her hand. Girl about your age. Red-haired chick." He opened the door, walked out into the stairwell outside our apartment.

I jumped up out of my chair, ran to the door. "Wait wait wait! Don't go!"

"Are you insane?" He was already in the stairwell, clumping down the stairs, a nasty grin on his face. "I'm not spending the rest of my life peeling your nutty mom off my shoulder."

"Wait, no, wait!"

He disappeared down the stairs.

"You've got to go to the police!" I called. "You have to tell them that I—"

"See ya," he called, his voice echoing distantly up out of the stairwell. "Wouldn't wanna be ya."

EIGHTEEN

"YOUNG LADY. YOU are *so* in trouble."

I don't know that I've ever seen my mom that mad.
It wasn't more than a couple minutes after the reporter
Troy Holliwell had left, and she was standing in the
doorway staring at me, her face all stiff and gray looking. Her hands were trembling. "So help me, God, Chass,
if you ever, ever, ever do that to me again . . ."

"Mom!" I said. "I'm sorry! But I—"

"Get in your room," she said. "Get in your room and
get your things. And maybe, just maybe, when we arrive

in whatever town we arrive in, I will have seen fit to forgive you."

I didn't move.

"Junebug, do you have any idea how that made me
feel? Spending the whole night out there, god only knows
where? You could have been dead for all I knew."

I just kept standing there.

"In your room," she said. "Now."

"I know who did it," I said. "I *really* know now."

"Chass." She was still trembling, and her voice was
very, very soft, like she was trying to keep from flipping
out on me. "Chass. I don't need to hear it. I need you to
go to your room and get your things."

I took a deep breath, then I sat down on the couch.

"Chass." She took a deep breath. "Don't. Make. Me.
Lose. My. Temper."

"Listen to me. What you're asking . . ." I tried to
think how to say this. "I've been with you all my life.
Running away from Kyle Van Epps. Losing friends. Losing my name. Putting up with a lot of stuff. It's not your
fault, Mom, it's just how it is."

She didn't say anything, just kept looking at me with
her eyes all cold.

"But please. Just for a minute think about what
you're asking. Someday—I don't know when, but *someday*—all this stuff between you and Kyle Van Epps will

be over. Maybe not this year, maybe not this decade. But someday."

Still she just kept looking at me.

"Mommy!" I hadn't called her Mommy in probably ten years. But for some reason it was all hitting me. I was feeling like a little kid again, needing somebody to hold me in their arms and tell me everything was going to be okay. "Mommy, I'm a suspect in a murder!" I could feel tears coming out of my eyes, running down my cheeks. "They have my fingerprints. If we leave town right now, this will follow me forever. I can't just pick up a new name and presto I'm a new person like we've done before. I won't be able to sing in public. I won't be able to get married. I won't be able to have kids. I won't be able to go to college or get a job that requires a background check. I'll be stuck on this same treadmill for my *whole life*! Mommy, please!"

Mom closed her eyes. Then she sat down next to me and put her face in her hands. I could hear her breathing.

Finally she said, "Chass, I just don't know what to do."

"Maybe it's time to stop running," I said.

"I don't . . . I don't . . ."

"Please. Mommy. There's got to be a better way. Please, Mommy! Help me."

She put her arms around me, and we started rocking back and forth and back and forth and back and forth, crying and rocking, like two little babies.

"What are we gonna do?" she said finally.

"I know who killed Josh Emmit," I said. "I just have to figure out a way to prove it."

"We just . . . we just don't have much time," she said.

"A day," I said. "I just have to figure out how."

We let go of each other then and sort of slumped back on the couch. I don't know how long we sat there, but it was awhile.

Suddenly there was a loud knock on the door, someone hammering on it with their fist.

We both jumped.

"Ma'am! Ma'am!" It was a man's voice. More banging. "I know you're in there. Open up!"

More banging.

"Ma'am! It's Inspector Wise, SFPD. We have an arrest warrant for your daughter!"

Suddenly Mom was all-business. "The fire escape," she said. "Go!"

"Ma'am! Don't make me break down this door!"

"I'm coming!" Mom shouted. Then she whacked me on the butt like I was a horse that she wanted to start galloping. "Now!"

She started walking toward the door. I ran for the bedroom window, yanked up the window. I could hear Mom in the other room, fiddling with the lock, trying to stall. I climbed out onto the fire escape. It seemed like a long way down. I hate high places.

I started going down as fast as I could. Just about the time I reached the first floor, a guy in a suit with a badge on his belt came around the corner at the alley behind the building. He spotted me, grabbed his walkie-talkie. "Subject is rabbiting!" he shouted into the walkie-talkie.

I started running back up the fire escape. Suddenly I didn't care how high I was.

Down below me I saw the detective drawing his gun.

"Stop!" he yelled. "Stop, now! Don't make me shoot you!"

Would he really shoot an unarmed sixteen-year-old girl? I wasn't sure. But I just kept running. The guy on the ground started cussing and yelling.

I ran past our window, kept going up the fire escape. The building was six stories high, which left two stories above our apartment. I thundered up the shaky metal stairway, which got shakier and shakier the higher I went. Finally it reached the rooftop. I climbed up, looked around. It was just a big flat space with some heating vents and a little concrete room with a door. This was the part where in the movies people always went jumping from rooftop to rooftop. I trotted around the edges, looking for someplace to go.

Our apartment building was next to another apartment building, about one story shorter than ours. I could hear somebody banging up the fire escape now.

I climbed over the lip of the wall leading to the building next to us, let go, sliding down the wall and skinning the crap out of my knees. Not that I really noticed. I ran over to the little concrete room that led down into the stairwell of the building next door. It was locked. I kicked the door. No luck. Solid steel.

I ran to the edge of the building, came to a screeching halt. It was five stories down to the ground. I ran to the other edge. Another five-story drop. I ran to the back of the building. Another five stories down. I was trapped.

I stopped, stared down. About fifty feet below me there were a couple of guys on a platform painting the building. It was sort of like what window washers used, hanging by ropes from the roof. What if I fell? Or jumped? I imagined the two painters, how surprised they'd be if some girl came sailing through the air past them. Or maybe I'd just fly by, there and gone in half a second, and they wouldn't even notice. A garbage can had been knocked over below them, spilling potato chip bags and orange peels across the sidewalk and into the road.

It's weird the stuff that crosses your mind at a time like that. I felt like my whole life was over. I'd always had all these big dreams. Dreams of going to amazing places and meeting cool people and playing music in front of huge crowds and driving a cool car with a great stereo system and marrying a really cool guy and having cool kids that were talented and smart, and living in a cool house with a swimming pool and a huge kitchen and a view of some beautiful lake or something . . .

And what if this was it? What if this was the high point, all downhill from here, standing on top of a cheap old apartment on some dirty street full of garbage? Behind me I heard Inspector Wise, calling down at me from the roof of my apartment building. "Give it up, Chass. It's over."

It's over.

The words were clanging around in my head. It's over. It's over. It's over. Everything I wanted to be, everything I wanted to do, everything I wanted to see—it was over. My whole life was over.

I stood there, swaying on the edge, and for about half a second all I could think was, Why not? Why not just jump? Save myself going through all the crap of being arrested for something I didn't do, prosecuted, probably convicted. Somebody in The Hundred would probably take credit for it, win the big prize, tell everybody how they'd framed me for something that I didn't do.

"It's over, Chass. Back away from the edge."

I imagined the red-haired girl, Clarissa Echols, laughing with all her cool friends, thinking how she'd gotten away with murder.

And suddenly I got mad.

I turned and looked at Inspector Wise. He was perched on the edge of the wall now, getting ready to shinny down to my location, his gun still pointed at me.

"Don't," I said. "Don't come down here."

"Or else what?" he said with a nasty smile. His round face was flushed, and he looked mad that I'd made him break a sweat.

I smiled back in what I hoped would look like a slightly crazy way. "Or else I'll jump, Inspector."

His smile faded a little. I moved half a step closer to the edge. From where I was standing I could see the big orange bridge leading over to Oakland. Mist was rolling in off the ocean over San Francisco Bay. It was a nice view.

"Okay okay okay, easy, hon," the inspector said.

I kept staring out at the city. The wind was gentle, and in any other circumstances it would have been really nice. But today it wasn't.

"So who was the rat?" I said finally.

"Huh?" the inspector said.

"The rat. Somebody called you and said that the gun was in my house. Was it a guy with a Ukranian accent?"

"I don't know what you're talking about."

"Oh, come on," I said. "What's the harm in telling me? My lawyer will find out eventually anyway. Somebody gave you a tip. I want to know who it was."

The inspector said, "You're not in a position to—"

And I sort of lunged toward the edge, like I was about to jump.

"Hey! Chass, hold on, hold on! I guess I could tell you."

I looked at the inspector and waited.

"It was one of your little buddies from The Hundred."

"Which little buddy would that be?"

"Neil Ostrov."

Somehow that didn't come as a surprise to me. "I have a question, though," I said. "Why were you talking to Neil Ostrov about Josh Emmit's murder?"

There was a brief silence. "He was a witness. He was sitting in the coffeehouse. He and Josh were supposed to meet."

"So . . . how did he know that the gun was in my house?"

"He says you showed it to him when he was at your house."

"Well, that's convenient," I said. "But given that he's never been over to my house, it's pretty much impossible."

"Save it for the jury," Inspector Wise said.

"Let me be clear on this," I said. "Neil Ostrov told you he was waiting for Josh in the coffeehouse."

"Yep."

"What about Will Gaffney?"

"Who?"

"Will Gaffney, Josh's friend. He told me that *he* was there waiting for Josh."

"I've never heard of anybody named Will Gaffney."

This was getting crazy. It seemed like everybody was lying about everything. I pulled out my cell phone, dialed Marco's cell phone number.

"Hey, Chass," he said. "Whattup."

"Nothing," I said.

"So you wanna sneak in some practice today?" he said.

"My schedule's a little hazy right now," I said. "Can I get back to you on that?"

"Sure."

"Meantime, you wouldn't happen to know where Annie is, would you?"

There was a short pause. "Actually? She's right here."

"I was hoping you'd say that. Can you put her on?"

After a second Annie came on the phone.

"So," I said. "You in the mood for showing off your driving skills again?"

"I don't know," she said. "What you got in mind?"

When I told her she said, "You're kidding right?"

"No," I said.

I could hear her breathing for a while as she was thinking about it. Finally she said, "Okay. See you in about ten minutes."

And that was that.

I looked over the edge. The painters were still down there three stories below me, completely unaware of my presence. The platform they were on dangled from wire ropes that were attached to motorized winches up on the roof.

I'm not one of these jock-type girls that's always trying to show the boys how tough I am and everything. I don't go rock climbing or rapelling. And I hate heights. In fact, I'm kind of a loser when it comes to physical stuff. So the idea of what I was about to do was not the sort of thing that would just pop into my head for fun. But I was in a really bad situation, and I figured there was only one way out.

Down.

My theory was that I could swing over the edge, grab hold of the wire rope, and ease myself down the side by grabbing the wire and pushing against the wall with my feet. I'd seen people do stuff like that in movies, so I figured if I just didn't look down, didn't panic, and kept moving, I'd be fine. Three stories to the painters' platform. That was twenty-five feet. How hard could that be?

It had to work, because if I fell, I would die. And dying was not an option.

So that's what I did. I took a couple of deep breaths. I felt like puking. My heart felt like it was going to explode, and for a second my vision got all gray and funny. But I kept saying to myself, *You have to you have to you have to you have to.*

And so finally I just did it: I swung my legs over the side, then grabbed hold of the wire rope, and prepared to ease myself down.

The thing about genius ideas is that a lot of times, they're not. Genius, I mean.

The second I let go of the lip of the roof and put all my weight on the wire was the second I realized just how greasy the wire was. I mean really, really, *really* greasy. Black, thick, gooey, gross, disgusting, incredibly slick greasy. So I had one of these Wile E. Coyote moments where I was like—*dude, this is totally not gonna work.* For a second it seemed kind of funny. Then the next second I was more scared than I'd ever been in my life. Because it didn't matter how hard you held that wire, you were just going to slide straight down it.

Which is what I did. I pretty much might as well not have been holding on to anything, that's how fast I was falling.

I had time to go, "Oh, shiiiiiii—" and there was this huge sickening crash and everything went black.

NINETEEN

I DON'T KNOW how long I lay there, but after a while I found myself looking straight up in the air. I was lying on a cool metal surface, and these two Mexican guys in white painters hats were looking down at me like I'd just fallen out of the sky.

Which, I guess, I pretty much had.

They looked at each other for a second and then started talking in Spanish to me.

I don't speak Spanish, and it was obvious these guys didn't speak any English.

After a little bit, I started to sit up, and the two guys grabbed my arms and helped me up. I sat there for a while, my head throbbing. Something was wrong with my leg too, but I wasn't exactly sure what. In fact, for a while I wasn't really sure *what* was happening.

Then it started coming to me.

"I need to go down," I said.

"Que?" one of the painters said.

"Down!" I pointed at the ground. "Down!"

"Down?" the painter said. His face was blank. He obviously had no idea what I was talking about.

"Down! I . . . NEED . . . TO . . . GO . . . DOWN!" Like if I yelled really loud and talked really slow they'd understand.

"Que?"

I was getting nowhere fast. I spotted a little control box at one end of the platform. It had some buttons and levers on it. I figured it had to control the winches on the roof. I stood up, hobbled over to the control thing, and grabbed a lever.

"No no no!" the painter said. And some other things that were probably like, *Hey you crazy idiot, don't mess with that or you'll kill us!*

I guess I should have listened, because the lever I pushed apparently only controlled one side of the plat-form. The wire on one side moved, and the left side of the platform lurched down about three feet. Suddenly we were not on a platform, we were on a slide.

All the paint, all the brushes, all the water, all the rags, all the lunch boxes and box cutters, and all the rest of the crap on the platform started going EEEEEEEEEE-EEEEEEEEEE, sliding slowly down the platform. The painters were trying to hold on to the sides and catch all the stuff before it slid off.

And while they were grabbing, they were yelling stuff at me that I didn't know what it meant, but I could tell it was not complimentary.

One of the guys was pointing at the box with the levers on it and yelling something and jabbing his finger. It hit me then that he was saying for me to use the other lever. If the left lever made the left side go down, then the right lever would make the right side go down.

Meanwhile I could hear shouting below us. The cop who had chased me up the fire escape was running down the road toward me.

"Get down from there!" he was yelling. "Freeze! Get down! Do not move!"

He reached the spot just below us when my fingers hit the second lever.

"Freeze! Come down here right this minute!"

"Well, dude, do you want me to freeze or do you want me to come down?" I said. "Make up your mind."

Sometimes it doesn't pay to be a smart-ass.

I was so busy coming up with my clever comeback line that I wasn't paying attention to what I should have been paying attention to. I guess I should have pushed the lever instead of pulling it. Because instead of making the right side of the platform go down, I made it go up. So now instead of a three-foot difference between the left side and the right side of the platform, there was about a five-foot difference.

All the stuff on the platform started falling—*shoomp, shoomp, shoomp, shoomp*—paint cans and brushes and buckets and everything, sliding past me and hitting the ground. As one of the paint cans pinwheeled through the air, big fat loops of white paint went sloshing off in all directions. One of them caught the detective right in the face.

He started yelling and staggering around.

"You foking idiote!" one of the painters yelled as I took a step, trying to keep from falling.

I understood him that time.

Unfortunately my foot hit a bunch of spilled paint and suddenly I had no traction at all.

This time there was no Wile E. Coyote time-stopping moment. One second I was standing on the platform, the next I was airborne.

As I fell, I saw a flash of purple out of the corner of my eye.

Purple meant Annie.

WHAM!

I landed on my feet, and a pain shot up through my leg, and I had this vague thought in my mind like, *Oh my god that's the most amazing pain I've ever felt in my life.* Worse than cramps, worse than the time my retard of a dentist in Spokane, Washington, forgot to give me novocaine before he started drilling my teeth, worse than anything I'd ever felt.

Then I was lying there on the ground, and the detective was staggering around like somebody out of a zombie movie, blind from the paint in his eyes, and people were yelling, and all kinds of stuff was crashing around me.

And one part of my brain was like, *Just let go. Just lie here and let go.* But some other part of my brain was telling me to get up.

All I could see from where I was lying was this sea of white. White paint was everywhere, splashed across the sidewalk and the cars and the overturned garbage can and the staggering, yelling detective. White everywhere. It was relaxing. Just let the world be white. Let it all go. Let it float away. Right?

And then something drifted into my vision, this flash of purple.

And something in the back of my mind was going, Get to the purple. Get up, and get to the purple.

And I'm going purple? white? purple? white? purple? white?

Who knows why you do anything, but for some reason purple won out. I got to my knees and started crawling toward the splotch of purple, and the pain in my leg was climbing up my chest and ringing around in my teeth, and the purple started to resolve into something, and finally I realized it was Annie's car.

I got up into a crouch, and the white figure of the detective started zombie-lurching toward me, pawing at his eyes, trying to see. I grabbed hold of a car, leaning my weight against it, then pushed off as the detective grabbed for me.

"Oh no you're not!" It was Annie yelling at me. I could see a look of horror on her face. "Girl, you are *not* ruining my upholstery with all that paint!"

Without thinking, I climbed onto the hood of her car, grabbed hold of the windshield wipers. I could see about three or four uniformed police tearing around the corner.

Five stories above me, Inspector Wise was pointing and yelling. "There! She's right there!"

"Go!" I yelled. "Go go go!"

Annie just kept staring at me.

"No you did not!" she said finally.

"Go!" I screamed.

"You did *not* just ruin my beautiful purple car with all that ugly ass white paint!"

"Go!"

The white-painted detective finally reached us. Instead of grabbing me, he reached through the window and grabbed the steering wheel. "Stop the car, ma'am," he said.

One little fleck of paint came off and got on the end of Annie's nose. She reached up with one finger, touched her nose—almost in wonderment—then looked at her finger like she totally couldn't believe what had just happened.

"Did you . . . did you . . . did you . . ."

"Did I what?" the detective said.

"Did you just get *paint* on my *face*?"

The detective glared at her, then reached out and ran his finger slowly, slowly, slowly down her face, leaving a wet white streak from brow to lips. "Yes, ma'am," he said. "I believe I did."

"Okay," Annie said to the detective. "See, 'cause I'm finally getting kind of pissed off."

And she floored it.

The tires threw up a bunch of smoke, and the car started to move. The startled detective let go of the steering wheel.

The next thing I knew we were flying down the road.

I flattened myself against the windshield, holding on to the wipers with all my might.

I don't know how long we drove, but it was way too long and way too fast to be going when you're on the hood of a car holding on to a couple of flimsy windshield wipers.

After a little bit, I turned my head and yelled, "Slow down!"

Annie didn't reply, didn't slow down. In the distance, maybe four blocks back, I saw a flash of blue lights.

We went around a corner. I was holding on for dear life. The wind was freezing cold, and my hands were starting to get stiff. If she kept this up, eventually my hands would get frozen and I'd be unable to hold on anymore.

"Just stop and let me off!" I yelled.

I might as well have been yelling at a wall. We wound around up and down and over and under. All I'd had in mind was for her to drive four or five blocks and then drop me off so that she wouldn't get in trouble with the police. But apparently she had other plans.

"Where are you going?" I yelled.

Still no answer. Annie's black eyes were focused on the road. I could hear sirens now. It seemed like they were coming from different directions, converging on us. I had this horrible thought that the cops would finally get us in sight and then Annie would feel obliged to do the same kind of crazy stuff she'd done the night before—all of it with me bouncing up and down on her hood.

Until I fell off and died, of course.

Suddenly we came around a corner and skidded into a filling station. Behind the filling station was one of those automatic car washes. Annie went sailing into the car wash without even stopping.

I was barely able to make out four or five police cars shooting by on the road next to us before I was nailed in the face by a jet of scalding hot water. I tried to sit up, but every time I moved I seemed to catch another blast in the face. Finally I just curled up and let the car wash envelop me in water. After a minute I sort of relaxed, and the warm water started to feel good. I hadn't realized just how cold I'd gotten.

And then it was over.

Annie pulled the car out of the washing bay and stopped. I rolled off the hood and lay on the tarmac, groaning and holding my ankle.

"I think my leg's broken," I said.

"I'm not talking to you," Annie said. Annie got a cloth out of the trunk and started drying off the hood of the car. "Poor baby," she said to her car. "Poor baby, that crazy girl got paint on you, but I saved you. Didn't I? Huh? Didn't I, baby? Yeah. Yeah, Mommy's here, baby. All the paint's gone."

She went on like that for a while. Finally I stood up, hobbled over toward the door.

"Hey!" Annie said. "No wet clothes inside my car!" She reached into the backseat, pulled out a gym bag, and threw it on the ground next to me.

I hobbled over to a Dumpster, opened the bag. There were some workout clothes inside. I peered around to make sure nobody was looking, then peeled off my wet clothes, stood there buck naked and dried off, then slipped into the sweat suit from the bag. When I was done, I looked around a second time to make sure nobody had seen me.

This time I looked a little more carefully. Next to the filling station stood a tall building that had a sign out front reading MILES STANDISH RETIREMENT CENTER. I scanned the back of the property, noticed there were some high concrete piers behind the place. At the top of the piers was a sunporch. And lined up along the porch were about six or eight old men, all of them in wheelchairs, staring down at me.

I stood there for a second, staring back at them, feeling like a total dork. Then I did the only thing I could think of: I curtsied.

The old men broke into a frail, thin burst of applause.

"Thank you," I said, doing my best Elvis imitation. "Thank you very much!"

TWENTY

NOW THAT I WAS dried off, I climbed in the front seat of Annie's car, called Marco again and asked him to find something out for me. He called back in about five minutes and gave me an address.

"Where you want to go?" Annie said.

"You still mad at me?" I said.

"Where we going?" she said.

"Three-five-three-five Clarendon Place. It's over near—"

"I know where it is," she said.

A few minutes later we pulled up in front of a large Victorian house on a tree-lined street. It was the sort of area where everybody drove a Volvo or Mercedes. "You mind if I do this myself?" I said to Annie.

She just shrugged. I guess she was still pissed about my getting paint on her car.

I walked up and rang the bell. After a minute a sort of severe, brittle-looking woman with red hair answered the door. Her pale skin was so thin and translucent it seemed like you could see right through to her bones. The resemblance to Clarissa Echols was so clear that it was obvious that the woman was Clarissa's mother. Her eyes were red-rimmed, like she might have been crying. "Yes?" she said sharply.

"Hi, Mrs. Echols," I said. I was trying to look relaxed and friendly instead of looking like I was about to pee in my pants. Which was how I really felt. "My name's Chass. I'm a friend of Clarissa's."

"Yes?" she said again.

"Could I talk to you for a minute?"

"This is not a good time," she said.

For a second I felt like just running back to the car. But I didn't. Instead I said, "Please. It's very important."

Mrs. Echols pursed her lips then finally stepped aside and let me into a beautiful living room. Lots of antique furniture, oil paintings on the wall, all the fabrics matching perfectly, not a speck of dust anywhere. No crumbs on the floor, no books or magazines stacked on the table, no dog hair, no worn spots on the rug. It looked like a Calvin Klein ad—everything so perfect that it came off totally fake, like a place that had been flash frozen in liquid nitrogen. Like it all might shatter if you touched it.

She gestured for me to sit on the couch. I wasn't even quite sure what I was doing here, what I was trying to find out.

"Um. I was wondering," I said. "Is Clarissa okay?"

She looked at me for a long time but didn't answer. She had her jaw clenched so that I could see all the tiny little muscles in her face. She sat across from me, balancing on the edge of the expensive-looking couch, her knees squeezed together like she was afraid some boy might try peeping up her skirt.

"Because there were a bunch of rumors going around at school."

Clarissa Echols's mother looked at me for a while. "Such as?"

"Like that she'd gone into drug rehab and stuff." I couldn't see any reaction at all. "I just wanted to check and see if she was okay."

"I didn't catch your name," she said.

"Chass," I said.

"Chass, I don't believe I've ever met you before," she said. "In fact, I've never even heard her mention your name."

"I just moved to San Francisco. We had started to get to know each other recently. She was nice to me once when she didn't have to be."

Clarissa Echols's mother pulled the corners of her mouth up without actually seeming to smile. She didn't say anything.

"I got the impression she was under a lot of stress lately," I said.

"That's putting it mildly," she said.

"I hope the rumors aren't true," I said. "I mean, I didn't get the impression she had a drug problem or anything."

"No. She doesn't."

Talking to this woman was like pulling teeth. "Is there someplace I could contact her?" I said. "You know, to offer some encouragement or whatever?"

"I'm afraid that's impossible."

"Not even e-mail?"

She just kept looking at me, not answering.

"She seemed really upset about Josh Emmit."

One red eyebrow twitched. "Are you a friend of his?" she said. "Are you one of *them*?"

"One of who?"

"I think you need to leave."

"Wait, wait, wait!" I said. "One of who?"

She stood quickly. "John! John!"

Nobody answered.

"John! Call the police! It's another one of those evil children!"

"Wait, wait, hold on!" I said. "I don't know what you're talking about."

She stood up and was looking around wildly, her hands shaking like leaves.

"Mrs. Echols," I said. "I don't know what you're talking about. I just wanted to . . ."

Mrs. Echols was breathing hard. She looked at me for a long time. "No," she said finally. "No, I suppose you're not one of them." She put her hands over her face and started to cry.

I went over to her and put my arm around her shoulder. She slumped against me and kept crying for a while. When she finally stopped crying, I said, "Look, I don't want to get into her business or whatever . . ."

She shook her head, then straightened up. Suddenly she looked all self-possessed again. She squeegeed one index finger under each eye, wiping away the tears and the muddy eyeliner.

"Josh did something to her, didn't he?" I said.

Her green eyes stared off into the distance for a while. "Yes. He did."

On the one hand, I wanted to comfort her. On the other I just wanted to pump some information out of her. It made me feel kind of dirty. I decided not to say anything, just to let her talk if she wanted to.

Mrs. Echols took another deep breath. "Did she ever tell you about this group she was in?"

"The Hundred?"

"So you've heard . . ."

"Just that it was some kind of creepy group she was in."

"Creepy isn't nearly good enough. Sick is more like it. It's a group of all these talented young people who get together each year and have a contest in which the goal is to victimize a member of the group."

I nodded.

"Last year," she went on, "my daughter was a cheerful, talented, happy, successful young person. A little high-strung maybe, okay. So she takes after me." She flashed a nervous, humorless smile. "Anyway last year, they had the contest. And the contest was to . . ."

She broke off and said nothing for a while.

"I can't even say it."

I just waited.

"Clarissa was raised a Catholic," she said finally.

"She's always been very committed to her faith. She was taught to believe that human life begins at conception, that abortion is murder. She . . ." Mrs. Echols stopped talking, took a long slow breath, then shook her head. "I can't. I just can't talk about it anymore.

"I can see in your face that you're a sincere girl," Mrs. Echols said. "Clarissa has always wanted approval. And so she's had a weakness for friends who were not very nice people."

I looked at the floor.

"I can see you're different, though," she said. "I don't suppose you're a Catholic?"

"No, ma'am."

"But if I . . . if you knew what happened to her, what she's gone through, would you pray for her?"

I'm not really the praying type. But what was I going to say? "Yes. I would."

She nodded curtly, as though she had made a decision. Then she stood and walked out of the room. After a while she came back and handed me a DVD in a plastic sleeve.

"Watch this," she said, handing me the DVD. "And then you'll understand why my daughter did what she did."

My heart suddenly started beating faster. "What *did* she do?"

"It's a sin," she said. "An unpardonable sin. I know that but . . ."

We stood there in silence for a long time. I felt like we were just hanging there on the edge. If I didn't breathe too hard, maybe she'd say it. *My daughter killed Josh Emmit. Just say it,* I kept thinking. *Just say it.*

"You'll pray for her, won't you? Promise me. God hears our prayers. I believe this with all my heart. If we pray hard enough, maybe he'll forgive her for what she's done. Promise me."

"Yes," I said.

She smiled, and for a moment she seemed like some kind of load had come off her shoulders. And I'm not sure, but I think I smiled too. Because I was sure in that moment that it was all about to come out—that Clarissa Echols shot Josh Emmit, that I had nothing to do with it, that I was just standing in the wrong place at the wrong time.

"Every day. You'll pray for her every day?" Mrs. Echols was gripping my hands now, squeezing them almost painfully.

"Every day," I said.

She hugged me. "You're a sweet girl, Chass," Mrs. Echols said. "She would have lived a lot longer if she'd had more friends like you."

I stiffened. "What?"

She released her hold on me. "I'm sorry," she said. "I should have told you earlier. She took a bottle full of sleeping pills. She was in a coma until about two hours ago."

"Wait . . ." I could feel the ground slipping away beneath me. "What . . ."

"I'm sorry, Chass. Clarissa is dead."

I stood there motionless. If Clarissa killed Josh, and Clarissa was dead, then there was no way for me to prove it.

"Pray for Clarissa," Mrs. Echols said. "Pray hard."

Then she put her face in her hands and rushed out of the room.

TWENTY-ONE

WE WERE ALL sprawled out in Fabe's apartment underneath his dad's huge house out in San Jose. He had a giant flat-screen TV hooked up to a DVD player and a humongous stereo.

"What is it?" Fabe said as I slid the DVD into the player.

"I don't know," I said. "Whatever it is, supposedly it explains why Clarissa Echols killed herself. And probably why she killed Josh Emmit."

I hit the PLAY button.

The shot that appeared on the screen was not very good. It was dark and wobbly. But still, you could make it out. It was a bunch of kids in masks, dancing, with a bunch of crappy techno playing in the background. Then it skipped to something else—a girl and a boy standing on a makeshift stage, both wearing Lone Ranger masks and long black cloaks. I recognized it as the stage in the warehouse where I'd been inducted into The Hundred. The video was shot from the back of the room, lots of masked kids milling around and talking.

"Okay, okay, hold it down guys!" the girl yelled. She had short, spiky brown hair.

"Guys, guys!" The boy waved his arms. He was a blond guy, very muscular.

Finally the kids settled down.

"All right, so the moment has arrived," the girl said. She cocked her hip, struck a little pose. One of these drama club types. "We have a winner!"

The kids cheered.

"As you know," the boy continued, "this year's contest was to get a girl in The Hundred pregnant and then make sure she had an abortion."

"The winner," the girl added, "is not the boy who gets her preggers, though. The way you had to win the contest was to be the person who *accompanied* the pregnant girl to the abortion clinic."

"Now, to present the winner, I'd like to randomly choose a member from among us who will award the prize to our big winner. Number Sixty-one, if you would be so kind."

He leaned over and picked up a trophy, held it out toward the girl. She reached in, pulled out a slip of paper. "Okay. And our award-giver-outer is . . . Number Eight. Number Eight? Come on up."

After a minute the crowd parted and a tall red-haired girl came up on the stage—somewhat tentatively. Despite her mask, it was obviously Clarissa Echols.

"Okay Number Eight," the boy said. "If you would please direct your attention to the stereo." Then he looked toward the back of the room. "Mr. DJ. Hit it!"

There was a loud hissing noise and then a voice spoke, staticky, as though it had been recorded on a cheap handheld tape recorder.

"I'm here for you," a loud voice said. A boy's voice.

Then something I couldn't make out. A sort of muffled sob.

"Don't worry about a thing. It's gonna be okay," the same voice said. He was trying to sound all sincere and comforting, but there was something about it that didn't ring true. I recognized it from somewhere.

On the stage Clarissa Echols' whole body seemed to

stiffen. She looked up at the speaker hanging over the stage, eyes wide behind her mask.

"I just—I don't know if I can do it." This time it was a girl's voice, thick from crying. I had a hunch it was Clarissa.

"Sure you can. You have to." And then I knew who it was. Josh Emmit. "Do you want to ruin your whole life? You're a talented, smart girl with everything in front of you. If you have this baby, you'll screw up everything."

"But it's wrong." Clarissa's voice was barely audible.

"I know, I know," Josh Emmit's voice said, booming out across the room. "But it's wrong for you to throw your life away too."

There was a long pause, some rustling and hissing.

On the stage Clarissa Echols tried to move, to flee—but before she could move, the girl in the black cloak put her arm around her, holding her fast.

"I just—" The girl's staticky voice again. "I just can't help thinking about that horrible contest."

A brief pause. "Contest? What contest?"

"In The Hundred. The contest. To get a girl pregnant, make them get an abortion. I mean, you're not going to tell anybody, are you?"

"Are you kidding me? You're my sister!" Josh Emmit

paused. More rustling. I imagined him putting his arm around Clarissa. "God, how could you even think that. I would *never* betray you."

All the kids laughed, and Clarissa Echols put her hands over her face.

The boy in the black cloak raised his hand. The hissing of the tape on the PA system stopped. "And the winner is . . ."

The girl with the spiky hair chimed in. "Number Fifty-three!"

Fifty-three. That was my number. Which meant the winner was . . .

Up in the front of the room, two masked boys high-fived each other. One was obviously Josh Emmit.

Josh Emmit leapt onto the stage, pumping his fists in the air. "Thank you! Thank you!" he yelled.

All the kids were cheering and laughing—all of them except Clarissa Echols, who was crying so hard that it looked like she was having convulsions.

"Let us recall the motto of our distinguished group," he called out loudly.

The kids all roared back: "TRUST NO ONE!"

"Hold on, hold on!" The boy in the black cloak held up his hand. "Lest we forget, guys, this contest is not just to find a winner. For every winner, there is a loser."

The crowed cheered and whistled.

"Ladies and gents, may I present to you," the girl with the spiky hair yelled, "this year's big-ass big-time loser, Number Eight!" She did a little Vanna White wave of her arm toward Clarissa Echols, who promptly collapsed to the floor, wailing horribly.

"Loser!" shouted the boy in the cloak.

"Loser! Loser! Loser!" The crowd started chanting.

On the stage, Josh Emmit started waving his arms back and forth, doing a little dance in time to the chant.

"LOSER! LOSER! LOSER! LOSER!"

I turned off the DVD player. I felt nauseated. There was a long hush.

"Okay, that is the sickest thing I've ever seen in my life," Marco said.

"So I guess it pretty much takes care of motive, though."

"Yeah," Annie said. "But the thing I'm wondering is—okay, let's say she killed Josh. Good for her. But how did the pistol end up in your apartment?"

"Will Gaffney's manager, that Ukranian guy, put it there," I said.

"Sure, but that's what I'm saying. How did her gun end up in his hands?"

"You know what?" I said. "I don't have the slightest idea."

"There's something we're still missing here," Fabe chimed in.

We all sat there for a minute thinking, when my cell phone rang. I thumbed the answer button. "Hello?"

"Dude!" a voice said. "Your band totally kicks ass!"

"Who is this?"

"It's your pal. Number Ninety-six," the voice said.

"Neil Ostrov," I said.

"So you remember we've got our big party tonight? We'll see who the big winner is."

I didn't say anything.

"Yeah, I hear a certain female member of our little group has apparently been charged with a major-league felony."

"What do you want, Neil?"

"I want you and your rockin' little combo to play at our party tonight." He had this dry, sarcastic tone, like he thought he was the funniest guy ever.

"Why should I do that?"

"Other than the fact that we'd pay you six hundred bucks?"

I sat there for a long time. It occurred to me that this was my last chance. There was one loose end here. The gun. Maybe I could worm something out of the arrogant jerk, something about how the gun came to be planted in my house. If I could find out that one thing, maybe, just maybe, I could get myself off the hook. Then again, maybe he would announce that he'd framed me and then two minutes later the police would bust down the doors and carry me off in handcuffs.

Truth was, I had run out of options. I had to take the chance.

"Eight hundred," I said.

"Done."

I had a sudden flash of inspiration. I needed to bait the hook. "Hey, by the way," I said. "I'm going to win the prize tonight."

"You are, huh? Gonna frame somebody for jay-walking?"

"Nah. For killing Josh Emmit."

There was a brief pause. "Yeah?" He was trying not to sound interested.

"There was a security camera tape from a store across the street from where he got killed. I managed to lay my hands on it."

Long pause. "I heard the cops tried to arrest *you* today," he said.

"Yeah, but that's before they saw this tape. I'm gonna play it for them tonight and they'll arrest somebody else instead of me."

"Who?"

"I guess you'll have to wait to find out."

"You don't win the prize if the person *actually* did it. They have to be framed."

"Who's to say whether they did or they didn't? Maybe the tape's a fake. All that matters is that tonight at midnight I'm going to give the cops some evidence that will get one of The Hundred arrested for murder." I smiled blandly. "See you tonight."

I hung up.

"A security tape?" Fabe looked puzzled.

"Listen," I said. "I have a plan . . ."

TWENTY-TWO

I ARRIVED AT the Triple X, a huge bar in the Mission District, around nine-thirty. The sign outside said BACK ROOM CLOSED TONIGHT FOR PRIVATE PARTY. Hip-hop was blasting out the door.

I walked in with my guitar. A guy in a black T-shirt scowled at me. "No kids in the damn bar," he shouted, hooking his thumb at the air.

"But I'm here for the—"

"Use the entrance off the alley."

I walked back outside and into an alley that led to the back room. There was an open door with a chain-link fence gate on it in place of a real door. I walked in. The back room of the Triple X was large, painted black, with ductwork and wires visible in the ceiling so that you felt like you were inside some huge black machine. I could hear the thud of hip-hop from the bar in the other part of the building. But this room was empty.

I walked toward the back wall, where there was a big stage with a nice sound system. I turned on one of the microphones. "Check, check, check," I said into the mic.

The sound of my voice, amplified, boomed out of the speakers. Fabe had promised me that he would come by early and make sure the sound system was all set up . . . but I just wanted to make sure. I strummed a few chords. My Takamine sounded great through the PA. I turned to the big rack of black electronic devices stacked up on the side of the stage, fiddled with some knobs to adjust my sound. As I was getting things adjusted, I heard something behind me, a metallic rattling noise.

"Can you play 'Oops, I Did It Again'?" a sarcastic female voice called out. "I love that song!"

"Yeah, right," I said, turning.

It was Neil Ostrov and his sidekick, Ingrid Leonard, the pale girl with the blond hair. They stood in the doorway for a moment, then Ingrid turned, closed the chain-link door, inserted a padlock into the hasp. It clicked loudly as she locked it. Instinctively I looked around the room to see if there were any other ways in or out. There was an emergency exit, but it was padlocked shut too. Suddenly I was feeling a little nervous about my brilliant plan.

"Hi, guys," I said, trying to sound cool. Then I turned back to my work, fiddling with the knobs on the rack of electronics.

I could hear footsteps approaching. I looked up again, and Ingrid Leonard had reached the stage. Neil was on the other side of the room now, sitting on a high bar stool and looking at me, his feet swinging back and forth. Ingrid leaned against the stage.

"So you think you're gonna win the contest today, huh?" she said.

I pressed a red button on one of the electronic devices that Fabe had told me about, a CD burner. Everything should be ready to go now.

"A tape of the murder," Ingrid said. "How convenient! It's amazing the cops didn't find it."

"It is, isn't it?" I said.

"Color or black and white?" she said.

"Color," I said. "Why?"

"Just wondering," she said. Then she reached in her purse, pulled something out, then leaned over. There was a flash of coppery red as she straightened up. She looked very different now that she was wearing a red wig. A lot like Clarissa Echols.

She must have seen the look in my eyes, the flash of surprise.

"I mean, it would have to be a really, *really* clear tape for somebody to be absolutely sure who did it." She smiled broadly. "Wouldn't it?"

"How did you know?" I said softly.

"Know what?" she said innocently. On the other side of the room, Neil Ostrov was smiling toward me.

"That it's a red-haired girl who committed the murder," I said.

She widened her eyes, pretending like I was telling her something really shocking. "A red-haired girl! Are you saying that Clarissa Echols killed Josh Emmit?"

"Or maybe it was somebody in a red wig," I said. "Like the one you're wearing."

Neil Ostrov hopped off his bar stool, sauntered over. "Look," he said, "we could chat about this all day. But the truth is, we just want the tape."

"Were you in it together?" I said.

"It doesn't matter," Neil said. Then he pulled out a

pistol and pointed it at me. The pistol in his hand looked a lot like the Russian gun that had been used to kill Josh Emmit.

My heart started slamming away in my chest. I looked frantically around the room.

"Both doors are chained shut," Ingrid Leonard said. "And there's really loud hip-hop cranking in the next room. You can't get out, and nobody will hear you if you scream."

"So we're pretty much gonna need the tape, dude," Neil said.

I looked at him for a long time.

Ingrid hopped up on the stage, put her arm around me like I was her best bud. "This doesn't have to get all personal and scary," she said. "Just give us the tape, we let you go."

"So it was you?" I said.

"Let's just say it was," Ingrid said. "Who cares?"

"You're gonna kill me, aren't you."

Ingrid sighed theatrically. "Yeah, sadly, I guess we pretty much have to."

"So what do you have to lose? At least tell me what happened."

"How dumb do you think we are?" she said. She strolled over to the CD burner in the PA rack, hit the EJECT button. There was a soft whir and then a gleaming

CD popped out of the tray. She picked it up and waved it in the air.

"You actually thought we'd come in here and confess to the murder?" Neil said.

The wind went right out of me. "I don't know anything about that," I said feebly.

"Sure you didn't," Ingrid said. "You didn't really think you could just turn all these microphones on and record us? Did you?"

"Well, it's irrelevant now," Neil said.

Ingrid dropped the CD on the ground, put one of her spike heels through it. It shattered, leaving a pile of gleaming shards on the dirty black rug.

"Enough screwing around," Neil said. "Give us the damn tape."

"No," I said.

Ingrid reached into her purse, pulled out a long, thin knife, ran it up the side of my face. "There are two ways we can do this. The duct tape and knives way. Which will be kind of slow and icky. Or the gun way."

"Which will be painless," Neil said.

I turned with trembling hands, opened my guitar case, pulled out a videocassette tape, handed it to Ingrid.

Ingrid handed it to Neil, who made a comical show of scrutinizing it. "Oh, yeah . . . no." Neil grinned, shook his head. "See, that's the wrong tape."

I didn't get what he was talking about. I frowned, puzzled.

"It's the tape," I said. "There's only one. It's yours. Please, just . . ."

"No," he said. "That's the point. We don't care about the murder at all. In fact, we had nothing to do with it, did we, Ingrid?"

"No, baby, we didn't."

I was growing more confused by the minute.

"Fact of the matter, there *is* a video," Neil said.

"And it shows quite clearly that you didn't kill Josh," Ingrid added.

"But first we'll need *your* tape."

"Okay, okay, guys—I'm totally confused," I said.

"The tape," Neil said.

"It's right there!" I said, pointing at the videotape in his hands.

He tossed it across the room. It smashed against the wall, fell on the floor with a soft clatter. "Nah, nah, not that tape."

"People are going to be here soon," I said. "You're not going to get away with this."

"Nobody's going to be here," Neil said.

"You're forgetting there's a party here tonight. People will start arriving here soon."

They looked at each other, pretending to be all puzzled. "What people."

"The Hundred," I said.

"Oh, yeah, that!" Ingrid said lightly.

"Yeah, see, the thing is?" Neil said.

"There is no The Hundred," Ingrid said.

I stared at them.

"Nah, The Hundred, that was sort of like . . ."

"Like theater," Ingrid said.

"Like a show."

"Like a movie."

"It looks real but it's not. It's all just made up."

I crossed my arms. "If you're through having fun, you want to tell me what you're really talking about?"

"Chass, Chass, Chass," a voice said behind me. It was a deep, grown-up voice, like one of those guys that does the voices on movie previews. I knew the voice. "You catch on slow, you know that?"

It couldn't be.

But it was. I turned, saw a middle-aged man, balding, with a little soul patch beard and a real expensive-looking suit. A nasty scar ran down the side of his face, twisting the left side of his mouth into a permanent smirk.

"You really thought you could get away from me?" the man said.

"Mr. Van Epps?" I said. "Are you saying . . . this whole thing was a setup?"

Ingrid ran the knife up the side of my face. "Oh, come on, Chass, he just wants the tape. Keep playing stupid, baby, because I really want to try out my new knife."

"Stop dicking around, Ingrid," Van Epps said. "Get her in the car before those kids in her band show up." Then he turned and started walking briskly toward the door.

TWENTY-THREE

THE TAPE.

How many times was this going to happen? Mom and I had been running from Kyle Van Epps my whole life. He wanted a tape, and we had it.

It was a tape that implicated him in a murder, a murder that happened a long time ago. If the tape ever surfaced, he'd go to jail. He had finally caught up with us a few months back. I had thought we were done with him for a while. But obviously I'd been wrong.

Half a minute later I was in the back of a long black limousine with tinted windows. The rear seats were set up facing each other. Neil had the gun jammed up against my ribs. Kyle Van Epps sat across from us next to Ingrid. A guy with dark sunglasses was driving.

"I don't see why you have to make this so hard," Kyle Van Epps said to me. "All I want is the tape. Give it to me and I'll leave you alone."

"You threatened my life before and I didn't tell you. What makes you think I'd tell you this time?"

Van Epps turned, snapped his fingers at the driver. The driver nodded and started moving.

"So I'm still confused," I said. "Who *did* kill Josh Emmit?"

"I had nothing to do with that," Kyle Van Epps said.

"Oh, come on," I said. "You might as well gloat, tell me how you set me up and all that stuff."

"I'm not going to gloat," Van Epps said. "However, I will explain what's just happened to you because that will help convince you to give me the tape."

"Yeah right."

"Just listen." The scar on his face twitched. "As you know, I'm the president of Apex Global Media Corporation. Josh Emmit was a recording artist for K-9 Records—which you have probably figured out is owned by Apex. After Josh was killed, my people naturally made it clear to the police that it was in their interest to keep us in the loop. Within a couple of hours, I found out that some girl singer named Chass had been a witness. Freak accident that you were where you were at the time. Point is, the word got back to me immediately. Once we knew that, we slipped a . . . ah . . . gratuity to Inspector Wise. He gave us a full debriefing about everything that he learned from you in the interview. The ingot with the numbers on it, the whole bit."

"Whatever."

"Look, I already know you're a tough kid. You don't have to prove it again." He touched the side of his ruined face. "This scar here is proof enough of that. What I'm getting at is that I decided this time around I wouldn't use the direct approach on you. What I figured was I needed to put you in some kind of hole. So I got a couple of screenwriters who were desperate to get in favor with me, sat them down, said, 'Here's what we know about what happened to Josh. Here's what we know about the part Chass played in his murder. Come up with a scenario that I can use to suck this kid in, put her under pressure so she'll give up the information I need.' They came up with the whole scenario—The Hundred, the numbered ingots, the nasty little game that The Hundred plays every year, blah blah blah. I admit, it was a kind of over-the-top plan. But what do you expect? They're writers."

"So the parties, the kids, Neil, Clarissa Echols . . ."

The driver of the car was moving swiftly through the city, making a lot more turns than seemed necessary to get where we were going.

"All fake. Actors. Neil's a real person. He really was Josh's best friend. But he's also an out-of-work actor who works as a part-time bookie to pay the rent. It wasn't hard for me to convince him to play ball with me. I told him I'd give him a major part in a movie, and he was ready to go. Anyway, after we got Neil on board, we approached Clarissa Echols to help us out. Again, Clarissa Echols is just a normal kid at your high school. She had delusions of being a movie star, so she was easy to convince too. Just like with Neil: I throw her a part in a movie, she does what I tell her. The idea was we'd sort of squeeze you in a vise with this murder thing, get you all paranoid about this Hundred group, wind you up with a lot of pressure . . . and she'd become your confidante. Then when the time was right, we'd manipulate the situation so that only the tape would get you out of the situation. She'd tell you that maybe you could trade the tape for your freedom. We hadn't quite worked that part out."

"But then things got a little weird," Neil said.

"Clarissa was nuttier than we realized," Mr. Van Epps continued. "She was kind of unstable, frankly. She

244

got all conflicted and freaky on us, started saying she'd go to the police and whatnot. It was not a good situation."

"Fortunately however . . . ," Ingrid added.

Neil finished her sentence for her. ". . . she couldn't take the pressure and offed herself."

Ingrid and Neil looked at each other, shared mean little smiles.

"Or maybe someone helped her?" I said.

Kyle Van Epps waved his hand. "Or maybe not," he said impatiently. "It doesn't matter. All that matters is that we get that tape."

"Hold on, hold on," I said. "I don't understand how you . . . The whole pregnancy thing? Her mom showed me this video."

"My people made the video. Part of the whole scenario we were putting you into. When things started looking bad for you, she was supposed to show you that video. Part of your chick-bonding experience, see? *We've both been screwed over by The Hundred, aren't we a pitiful pair, blah blah blah.*"

I frowned. "But . . . that's not possible. Josh Emmit was in the video."

"You ever heard of a body double? You need a close-up shot of an actress's butt for a movie. But your actress has been eating too many doughnuts and her buns need a little lipo? No, problem. You get a body double, a girl with a nice tight body, shoot her ass instead. Remember, the guy you thought was Josh in the video? He was wearing a mask. You never saw his face."

It seemed like he had an answer for everything. And yet, it was hard to believe he'd gone to all this trouble. "But Josh said, 'Stop The Hundred.' He must have meant *something*."

Van Epps shrugged. "The working title of his new album was *The Hundred*. Title track was going to be a song about hundred-dollar bills. Hey, look, the guy was dying. Who knows what he meant. Probably nothing."

I felt sick. I couldn't believe I'd been taken in by this whole thing. "So what now?" I said.

"Well, it's not as theatrical as the scenario my writers had in mind, but the bottom line here is the same. You're about to go down for murder. And we can stop that from happening."

"How?"

"Simple. We know that you don't have a surveillance video of the murder."

"Oh really," I said. "And how would you know that?"

"Because my people looked at every surveillance tape in the entire neighborhood." He smiled crookedly.

"And . . . ," I said.

"And we found one. A real one."

Neil chimed in, "A video that proves what really happened."

Ingrid added, "And Mr. Van Epps has the only copy."

The limo took a sudden left turn, throwing me into Neil's lap. I heard horns honking and a big truck zipped by our trunk, narrowly missing us. It looked as though Kyle Van Epps's driver had intentionally blown through a red light. Probably to throw off anybody who might be following us.

"How'd you get the video?" I said.

"I had twenty private investigators on this thing before I even knew about you—just because Josh was one of my top artists. The cop on this case is not an idiot—but he just doesn't have the manpower I do. I found a surveillance camera across the street. They burned us a DVD of it. My investigator then made sure the whole thing was erased from their hard drive. There's a clear shot of the killer's gun coming out of the car." He held up a gleaming DVD. "And I've got the only copy of it."

"The corner of Fillmore and Eddy," I said.

"What?"

"That's about half a block from where the storage warehouse is," I said, "the one where the tape that you want is. But I'm not telling you which locker it's in. Not till I see the DVD."

Mr. Van Epps nodded at Neil, who hit a button in the door of the limo. A flat-screen TV folded down from the ceiling. Neil slid the DVD into the machine and a grainy video began playing. The front door of a store dominated the screen. But way off in the background, across the street I saw . . . me. It showed me taping the picture on the window of the coffeehouse. Then Josh Emmit coming up behind me.

Suddenly I felt clammy and sick to my stomach, knowing what was about to happen. For a moment it was like I was there all over again, the whole thing playing over in my mind.

Then a car pulled up near the curb behind Josh Emmit. It was impossible to see in the windows because of the glare. Then a hand reached out the window. I knew there had to be a gun there, but I couldn't make it out. Then there was a flash coming out of the hand. And another. Josh Emmit slumped down, and the car pulled out into the road. As it was pulling out, another car, a red car, had to slam on its brakes to stop. *Oh my God,* I was thinking. *There had been a second car. I hadn't even noticed it.* The second car was the one that I noticed. I must have been distracted by Josh. Then when I looked up the red car with Troy Holliwell in it drove off. And so I thought the shots had come from inside the red car. My breathing sped up and for a second I thought I might faint.

"Turn it off," I whispered.

"I think you'll agree, it's enough to get the charges against you dropped."

Neil Ostrov hit the STOP button. On the screen was a frozen shot of a blond girl, leaning forward, getting ready to run. It looked like she was about to topple over. The girl on the video seemed halfway like me. And yet, she seemed halfway like a total stranger.

"What I don't get is how the gun got in my house. If you didn't have anything to do with the murder, how did you get your hands on the gun?"

"I'm getting bored with this," Mr. Van Epps said.

"The corner of Fillmore and Eddy," I said.

"Huh?" Van Epps said.

"The corner of Fillmore and Eddy," I said again. "We're going to the corner of Fillmore and Eddy."

Kyle Van Epps narrowed his eyes. "You already said that."

"I told you we were going to the corner of Fillmore and Eddy?"

Kyle Van Epps studied my face for a minute. Suddenly his eyes hardened. "Son of a—"

He reached across the seat and ripped open my

blouse. I didn't even have time to be scared. Mr. Van Epps stared at my chest. But it was obvious he wasn't interested in my boobs. What he was looking at was the little microphone planted at the base of my bra.

"What?" Neil said.

Mr. Van Epps reached over and yanked the microphone off my chest. He held it up in front of Neil's face.

"She's wired. It's a trap. She kept saying the corner of Fillmore and Eddy so that whoever's listening in would know where we were going."

"But—" Neil's eyes widened. "The CD burner over at Triple X . . ."

"That was just a distraction," Van Epps said. He rolled down the window, threw the mic out onto the street. "She wanted you to think you were smarter than her once you found the CD in the burner. Then you'd drop your guard."

We drove down the street for a couple of blocks, no one saying a word.

"What are we gonna do, boss?" Neil said finally. "Should we waste her?"

"We don't know who's on the other end of the wire, you idiot," Mr. Van Epps said. "It could be the cops. If we killed her, who do you think would be the first suspects? Huh? Huh, genius?"

"Then what—"

"Stop the car!" Kyle Van Epps barked.

The driver slammed on the brakes.

"Dump her," Van Epps said.

"Excuse me?"

"Open the door and dump her. Now!"

Neil opened the door, grabbed me by the arm. As he pulled me forward, I slammed my hand against the DVD player. The tray slid open. I reached for the DVD. Neil grabbed my hair and yanked viciously. I screamed as a sheet of pain tore across my scalp, forcing me to more or less hurl myself out the door.

I landed in a heap in the gutter, my shoulder smashing against the steel grate set into the concrete.

The last thing I saw before the limo sped off was Kyle Van Epps's face. "You got lucky this time," he said, a hard smile on his face. "I *will* get that tape. Guarantee it."

The door slammed and the limo's tires screeched. Within seconds it was gone.

I looked around me. It was not the most fabulous neighborhood. A couple of cars zoomed by.

Kyle Van Epps had been right. The reason I had repeated the address we were driving to was so that Fabe, Annie, and Marco were going to be there waiting for me. Fabe, with all his electronic recording gear, had used a cordless stage mic to manufacture a makeshift wire like the kind used by the FBI. But he had cautioned me that it had a fairly short range so I should repeat anything that was important a couple of times in case the signal broke up.

I hoped that Fabe was following close behind the limo so they could pick me up. But as I looked up and down the street I realized that somehow Van Epps's driver must have lost them. That was probably why he had blown through the red light earlier: he was making sure nobody was tailing us. Whatever he had done, it had worked: I didn't see Fabe's BMW or Annie's purple car anywhere.

Another car, however, was slowing in front of me.

I sat up and uncurled my hand. Inside it was a DVD. I smiled. Well, at least this would get me off the hook.

The long black car stopped in front of me, the door opened quickly, and a young man stepped out.

"Will?" I said, surprised. It was Will Gaffney. "What are you doing here?"

"Hop in," he said, smiling. "I'll give you a ride."

I kept looking at him, trying to figure out why he was here.

"Come on. Hop in."

I walked around, opened the door, but didn't get in. I couldn't quite figure out what was wrong. But something made me not want to get in the car. He sat in the driver's seat, then reached across, grabbed my arm and pulled me in. I sat there for a moment, the DVD in my lap.

He floored it, and the car moved back into the road.

"Let me guess," he said. "The DVD. Is that Mr. Van Epps's security tape of the murder?"

"Uh . . .," I said.

"I thought so," he said.

His smile went away. He reached over, opened the glove box, pulled out a gun. "I'll take that." He scooped up the DVD from my lap.

I stared at him. "You?" I said. "It was *you*?"

TWENTY-FOUR

WILL GAFFNEY DROVE for a few blocks and then I said, "You know what, how about you drop me off up here. I feel like walking."

"Nah, nah, nah," he said. "This is a bad neighborhood. I wouldn't dream of letting you out here."

"Seriously I—"

"Cut the crap, Chass," he said, pointing the gun at me. "I'm not letting you out of this car. Not alive anyway."

I was so wrung out I barely even felt scared. More numb than anything else.

254

"Why?" I said finally.

"Why what?"

"Why did you kill Josh?"

"Because he was trying to take my dreams away from me."

"What's that mean?"

"He was so full of himself. It was all about him. Always. All about him." Will's face was impassive but his voice was full of venom. "He was afraid of me, see? He was afraid I was better than him, that I was gonna shove him aside, take his place at the table, knock him off the charts. He was undermining me with the record company, bad-mouthing me to Mr. Van Epps and the other record company executives. I told you I had a development deal right? Well, it was about to be canceled. No CD, no contract, no money, no nothing. They were gonna drop me cold. And it was all because of Josh. But I knew that if I played the new track for them, they'd change their minds."

"You killed him for a *song*?"

"It was Josh's fault! All he had to do was give me my track and I'd have left him alone."

"So you just rolled up on him and shot him?" I said.

"He was robbing me of my dreams. That's not right."

"And then you had your manager plant the gun in my house."

He shrugged. "That was Mr. Van Epps's idea."

"You mean he knew that you killed Josh?"

There was a long pause. "The minute he found out Josh was dead, he called me. He was like, 'You did it, didn't you?' I mean, I tried to deny it but . . . Mr. Van Epps, man, he's a kinda persuasive guy."

I thought about it for a while.

"You wore a red wig in the car," I said.

"Until I was six years old, my mom dressed me up like a girl. Nobody ever knew the difference."

"That's a little creepy."

"That's nothing. She did things . . . stuff that was a lot creepier than that." He took a deep breath, seemed to be willing himself to relax, smiled. "But I'm over that now. I'm moving on."

"Good for you," I said. He didn't seem to get the sarcasm.

"I had to wear some kind of disguise in case I got spotted when I was shooting him. I bought the wig at a costume shop over in the Castro." He frowned. "Anyway, how'd you know I wore the wig? Oh, wait, no—it's on the DVD, right?"

"The DVD doesn't even show your face," I said. "It just shows a hand coming out of a car, pointing the gun."

"Oh, that's nice to hear. Still, it's a little inconvenient. There's probably some kind of clue on there that would implicate me. The license plate, the kind of car I was driving, something. I'd sure hate for the cops to get their hands on this."

He grinned, rolled his window down, tossed the disc out the window. I turned and watched it bounce a couple of times, then roll down the street before disappearing into a storm drain. Which is when I realized what I had to do.

I reached down, put my seat belt on.

"What," Will said, "you afraid I'm gonna get in a wreck and get you killed?" He snickered.

"Something like that," I said.

Then I grabbed the steering wheel and cranked it with every ounce of strength I had.

"What the—" Will fought me for control of the wheel, but by then it was too late.

His big car crossed over into oncoming traffic. Horns blared, brakes screeched, then there was a parked car swimming up in front of us.

Will slammed on the brakes. There was a horrible smashing thud. I could hear metal ripping. Then everything was black.

TWENTY-FIVE

WHEN I CAME to, I was upside down. It took me a minute to figure out what was going on. I could hear something dripping and sizzling, and I could smell gas. The withered cloth of an air bag dangled in my lap. It all seemed kind of strange and inexplicable. Finally I remembered what had just happened.

I unhooked the seat belt and fell down. Everything hurt—my arms, my legs, my neck, and especially my face and chest, where I'd smashed into the air bag. On the other side of the seat I could see Will, all crumpled up underneath the dashboard. He hadn't been wearing his seat belt, so the air bag hadn't helped him much. I guess he must have slid under it on impact, and his legs had folded up like pretzels as he smashed into the underside of the steering wheel. My purse had popped open and all my stuff was spread out all over the roof of the upside-down car. Tampons, mascara, blush, lipstick, pennies, chewing gum, the ingot—they were scattered everywhere.

Will was still conscious. I could see his eyes following me. He didn't say anything, though, and his face was a sickly white. His right hand moved slowly, feeling its way across the roof of the car like a little animal. He touched the tampon pouch, then the lipstick, then the ingot. His hand stopped. He picked up the ingot, looked at it, blinked.

The roof of the car had collapsed and the window was smashed out. Where the window had once been a foot and a half high, it was now about six inches. I didn't think there was any way I could get out. I could still hear the dripping and sizzling noises from the direction of the motor.

Will kept looking at the ingot. Then he got this sour smile on his face. "Why?"

"Why what?"

"Josh. He gave. Ingot. To you. Why?"

The dripping and sizzling noises continued from inside the motor compartment.

Will's eyes widened. He whispered something that I couldn't make out.

"What?" I said.

"Gas," he whispered.

"Huh?"

"That dripping sound," he whispered. "Gas."

"Oh," I said.

"The gas. Is gonna. Hit something. Hot. In a minute. Then the car's. Gonna. Blow." He was having a hard time breathing.

I just lay there in a ball.

"Help," Will said. "Don't let me. Die. In here."

I decided I better make an attempt to get through the window. But before I moved, I grabbed the ingot from his hand. He resisted for a moment, then let go. I don't know why I wanted it. But I did. Then I poked my head out the crumpled window. The air felt nice and cool on my face, and for a minute I just lay there. My arms didn't seem to have any strength. Finally I rallied. I pulled and wriggled and wriggled and pulled. It was very very tight. I could feel broken glass ripping at my clothes and my skin.

"Help." It was Will, whispering inside the car. His voice was so soft I could barely hear it.

I managed to get out.

"Help."

People were surrounding me now, asking me what happened, asking me if I was all right, shouting questions at me that didn't seem to make any sense.

"Help." I wasn't even sure if I was hearing Will's whisper or whether it was in my mind.

I began stumbling back down the road.

"Where are you going?" somebody yelled.

"Is there anybody else in the car?"

I didn't answer. My eyes were fixed on the storm drain at the far end of the street.

"Hey! Hey!"

I just kept walking.

"Help." I could still hear Will whispering to me. "Help."

By the time I reached the storm drain I was pretty sure it was just in my head. I saw something glassy and gold lodged in a tangle of potato chip bags and rotten leaves beneath the steel bars of the grate. I lay on the road and reached my arm all the way into the storm drain. There it was, something cool and smooth against my fingers. My fingers closed around the DVD.

As I pulled it out of the drain, I heard a loud *whoosh*, like a giant sucking on a milk-shake straw. Then Will's car went up in flames.

"Help," the voice whispered, coming up out of the blackness of the drain now. "Help."

TWENTY-SIX

AN HOUR LATER we were out at Fabe's, sitting in the studio in his basement. "So, look," I said. "This is it."

"What's it?" Marco said.

"We can play one last song, then I'm gone."

The members of my band stared at me, puzzled.

"I can't get into it now," I said, "but my mother and I have to leave town tonight. She's on the way out here right now."

"But . . . what about the DVD?" Annie said. "Doesn't it prove you're innocent?"

I nodded. "That's not why I have to leave, though. There's a guy who's after me and Mom. We can't stay in San Francisco."

"But . . ." Marco's eyes widened. "But, Chass, this band is a sure thing! I can feel it in my bones!"

I felt tears stinging my eyes. "I know," I said. "I can too."

Fabe was drumming on his leg, staring up into the air with an empty expression on his face. Annie just looked mad.

I strapped on my guitar, started playing a song I'd written called "Good-bye Sucks." I'd written it after leaving Alabama.

Everybody laughed, and somehow the mood shifted a little. Marco sat down behind the keyboard, started playing a couple of fills, then Annie plugged in her bass, and away we went.

We played the last chorus about five times, none of us wanting to let it go. I might have expected Annie or Marco to get all emotional, but I was surprised when we finished to see tears running down Fabe's face.

I started packing up my guitar.

Everybody came over and gave me a hug, first Annie, then Marco, and finally Fabe. "This band . . . ," he said to me. "This band is the most *right* thing that's ever hap-pened to me."

I nodded. *Me too,* I was thinking. "Maybe so," I said. "But I have to go, and I can never see you again."

I reached into my purse, took out the ingot with the number fifty-three stamped in it, held it out to the group. "Here," I said. "Something to remember me by." Marco and Annie both reached for the ingot. Their hands banged together, and the ingot fell on the ground. Fabe leaned over, squinted at it curiously. I started to go, but then he said, "Hey. Check this out."

"What?"

He held up the ingot so I could see. When it had hit the ground, a little panel had slid back on the top—revealing the controls of some kind of electronic device.

"It's an iPod," Annie said.

I looked at it. Sure enough, hidden inside the ingot was an MP3 player.

"Why would Josh have given that to me?" I said. "That's a pretty weird thing to do when you're about to die."

Fabe frowned, leaned forward. "Let me see that for a sec." He walked around to the control panel for his studio, fished some wires out of a drawer, plugged one end into the iPod, the other into the patch bay of his studio. He sat at the computer screen, hit a few keys. "I'll be damned, look at that," he said.

I came up behind him, looked at the screen. It was a list of songs from the MP3 player. "So?" I said.

"A normal iPod would have all the songs listed by name. And the files would all be in MP3 format. The stuff on here isn't like that. The files are just numbered. See, every single file name starts with the number 100. And all the terminators are wrong. These are ProTools format."

"Try talking to me in English," I said.

"These are tracks from a multitrack master recording. The masters he stole from his record company? He downloaded them onto his iPod. He was carrying his whole record in here. Along with the song Will was trying to get hold of."

"Oh my God. So Will had it in his hand. He had what he wanted and didn't even know it." Then it hit me. "I just realized something. When he was dying, Josh didn't say, 'Stop the hundred.' He had said, 'Stop. The Hundred.' Two separate sentences. He was just telling me to stop, not to run away yet. He must have been trying to tell me that his record, *The Hundred,* was in his iPod. I guess he thought whoever was shooting him was sent by Mr. Van Epps—that it had something to do with his contract dispute with the record company. So he was giving me the record to try and keep the master away from Mr. Van Epps."

As we were talking the doorbell rang.

Fabe opened the door. Mom was silhouetted in the light, watching us. I handed Fabe the DVD that proved I hadn't killed Josh Emmit. It was packed in an envelope with Inspector Wise's name and address on it. I'd written a short note to accompany it, explaining what had happened, how Will had killed Josh Emmit and why. "Mail this for me?" I said.

"Sure."

I gave him a last hug.

"We're going to find you, you know, Chass," Fabe whispered into my ear. "This band is not gonna die."

"You can't," I said.

"No, you don't understand," he said. "We're *going* to find you."